"An amusing, brittle, sensible comedy of parents and children, displaying the gulf between the prudishness of the younger generation and the flightiness of their elders."
—*Daily Telegraph*

"This interplay of imagination is what makes reading Henry Green so rewarding; there can be few novelists who give such line by line pleasure."
—*Times Literary Supplement*

"*Nothing* has that air of effortlessness that conceals the polish of the art that has gone into its making."
—*New York Herald Tribune*

"Beneath the pleasant surface of Mr. Green's 'light' fiction there is a strikingly bold intelligence and an acute knowledge of this wayward world. Maddeningly accurate, endlessly suggestive."
—*New York Times Book Review*

"A funny book, one that all but the most crabbed readers will laugh at from start to finish. . . . Mr. Green is an absolutely original stylist."
—*New Yorker*

"Deft, adroit, unfailingly amusing."
—*Saturday Review*

"*Nothing* may be well named for some, but for this reader it is technically and brilliantly something! Remarkable."
—*Chicago Tribune*

"A pointed poke at solemn youth, but the poke is so obviously accompanied by so many friendly winks that even its victims will enjoy it."
—*Time*

"Brilliantly observed. No one can write dialogue as he can. A very remarkable novel."
—*Observer*

BOOKS BY HENRY GREEN

NOTHING

HENRY GREEN

Dalkey Archive Press

First Dalkey Archive edition, 2000

Library of Congress Cataloging-in-Publication Data:

Green, Henry, 1905-1974.
        Nothing / by Henry Green. — 1st Dalkey Archive ed.
              p. cm. — (British literature series)
        ISBN 1-56478-260-3 (acid-free paper)
        1. Conflict of generations—Fiction. 2. Parent and child—Fiction. I. Title.

PR6013.R416 N6 2000
823'.912—dc21   00-058953

Partially funded by a grant from the the Illinois Arts Council, a state agency.

Dalkey Archive Press
www.dalkeyarchive.com

Printed on permanent/durable acid-free paper and bound in the United States of America.

NOTHING

O N A S U N D A Y A F T E R N O O N in nineteen forty eight
John Pomfret, a widower of forty five, sat over lunch with
Miss Liz Jennings at one of the round tables set by a great
window that opened on the Park, a view which had made
this hotel loved by the favoured of Europe when they visited
London.

He did not look at the girl and seemed nervous as he
described his tea the previous Sunday when Liz had to visit
her mother ill with flu so that he had been free to call on
Jane Weatherby, a widow only too well known to Miss
Jennings. It was wet then, did she remember he was saying,
so unlike this he said, and turned his face to the dazzle of
window, it had been dark with sad tears on the panes and
streets of blue canals as he sat by her fire for Jane liked dusk,
would not turn on the lights until she couldn't see to move,
while outside a single street lamp was yellow, reflected over
a thousand rain drops on the glass, the fire was rose, and
Penelope came in. Jane cried out with loving admiration and
there the child had been, no taller than the dark armchair, all
eyes, her head one long curl coppered next the fire and on
the far side as pale as that street lamp or as small flames
within the grate, and she was dressed in pink which the
glow blushed to rose then paled then glowed once more to
a wild wind in the chimney before their two faces dark
across Sunday afternoon.

"Then you're to be married" Jane had cried and so it was
he realised, as he now told Miss Jennings, that the veil of
window muslin twisted in a mist on top of the child's head
to fall to dark snow at her heels, with the book pressed

I

between two white palms in supplication, in adorable humility, that all this spelled marriage, heralded a bride without music by firelight, a black mouth trembling mischief and eyes, huge in one so young, which the fire's glow sowed with sparkling points of rose.

"Oh aren't you lucky" Jane said, "you sweet you?" but the infant said no word.

It was then he fell, he told Miss Jennings. He had gone on his knees. Not direct onto the floor, he explained. No, he used one of those small needlework cushions women put about a room and the fact was Penelope made no objection when he suggested the ceremony should take place at once. There was a cigar band handy in the ashtray for a ring and he had, he swore it, looked first at Jane who'd only said "why not then darling?" Thus it is he explained to Miss Jennings that the great mistakes in life are made. And it was Jane, he went on, had called "wilt thou take this man?" while the little girl stayed agreeably silent, had continued "for richer or poorer, for better or for worse" right through her own remembered version of the service. Or perhaps Jane had altered the words to make it unreal to herself, Mr Pomfret did not know he said. But the harm was there.

He came out of his description to find Miss Jennings laughing.

"Oh my dear" she gasped "you should never be allowed to play with small children. Particularly not little girls!"

"I know, I know" he said.

"So when did the tears start darling?"

He objected that Jane had not cried then and went on to explain that so soon as this mock ceremony ended and Penelope had flown to her mother's arms he'd taken it all a fatal step forward and asked the child to sit on her husband's knee.

"You see they made an absolute picture" he explained. "You know what Janie's eyes are with that wonderful blessing out of the huge things."

"Well?" Miss Jennings demanded when he paused.

"Just look at the man over there Liz I ask you" he temporised. "Where was I? Oh yes" and went on to describe Penelope's little face buried in Jane's bosom. He'd made a further invitation on which Jane did not call him to order, then suddenly, he said, it broke, there was a great wail came out with a "Mummy I don't want" after which nothing was any use, all had been tears.

"I nearly sobbed myself. Oh the blame I had to take! No but seriously you can't think it wrong of me Liz?"

"Are you seeing a lot of Jane these days?" Miss Jennings wanted to be told.

"She's supposed to lunch here this very afternoon" he answered. "Which is as much as I ever see her, once in a blue moon, except when you choose to go sick-nursing."

"Mother isn't often . . ." she began.

"My dear what's come over you" he interrupted, "I wasn't serious. No but do look over that man again. Well as you can imagine" he proceeded "it's gone on ever since. Whenever I ring I get the latest the child has imagined, she simply never seems to sleep now at all isn't it awful, and the little boy who comes to tea with her quite heartbroken; Liz do say you don't think it was dreadful of me!"

"What man did you mean?"

"Over there with a wig and the painted eyebrows."

"Oh no how disgusting. But I can't see anyone even remotely like! Well go on. This story of yours begins to amuse me rather, darling."

"There's no more. But look here Liz you can't think it was indecent can you now?"

"Not a very nice thing after all."

"But I couldn't tell how she would react to sitting on my knee could I?"

"You should never have married her."

"Yes but Liz she didn't once in practice settle on my knee."

"That's not the point dear. Now Jane won't ever hear the last!" Miss Jennings sniffed. "Well you said she was due and

here she comes. We've simply talked her into the room!"
Liz made a face as he craned to see Jane.

"Still Dick Abbot" Mr Pomfret remarked of the man
with her. "Hello there" he waved. With a great smile and
one or two nods that seemed to promise paradise, Mrs
Weatherby changed course, made her way between tables
to kiss Liz, to lay with a look of mischief and delight
between John's two palms a white hand which he pressed
as had her own child the imaginary psalter.

The two women greeted one another warmly.

"And how's Penelope?" he asked in his most indifferent
voice.

"She's just a little saint" the mother answered. "Oh
weren't you wicked! I suppose he's confessed to you Liz?
Isn't it simply unbelievable!" But she was smiling with great
good-nature.

"Have you heard about poor old Arthur?" John enquired.

"Arthur Morris no" Jane said, her face at once serious,
the eyes great and fixed.

"Only a simple nail in the toe of his left shoe" John told
them. "A small puncture in the ball of the foot. But they've
had to take the big toe off and now he's dangerously ill."
He looked up at Jane. Her eyes grew round.

"Oh no," she said, then began to shake. She was soon
helplessly giggling without a sound. Then it spread to Liz
and she clapped a hand over her mouth above blue eyes that
watered with silent laughter.

"They may even have to amputate the ankle" he added
smiling broadly now.

"His ankle?" Jane cried, a tremor in her voice. Miss Jennings' shoulders began to heave. "Forgive me I can't help
myself. Dick have you heard?" Mrs Weatherby called out
and turned around as though the escort must be close
behind. He was nowhere near.

"But how rude of Richard!" she exclaimed, serious again
at once.

Dick Abbot at that moment was in conference with a

youthful seeming creature dressed up in the gold braid of a hotel porter and who turned away to bully a head waiter in white tie and tails.

"Table trouble" John said.

"I ought to be on my way I suppose" Mrs Weatherby announced then began her farewell smile. "Goodbye darling" she murmured as if to promise everything again.

"The Japanese do" Mr Pomfret explained to her back.

"Do what good God?" Miss Jennings demanded.

"They all laugh even when their very own are at death's door. It's nerves. You don't think that dreadful surely? Once Jane starts I've as much as I can do to stop myself."

"She's rather sweet" Liz said "though I say as shouldn't."

He seemed to ignore this.

"The young don't laugh" he complained.

"I do, I can't help it" she said.

"They don't" he insisted gloomily.

"So what about me?" asked Miss Jennings, all smiles.

"I love you" he said smiling back. "That's one reason I love you Liz."

"Well then? We've been over every one of your other friends haven't we? And lunch Sunday's as much as we ever seem to have. So let's talk about me."

"Oh don't mention Sunday darling please, that brings up tomorrow, our all inevitably going back to work. Why it's too despairing," and his voice rose, "too too awful" and he flapped both hands, "like a dip into the future, every hope gone, endless work work work!"

The man in porter's uniform close by hurried across upon these gestures, a head waiter in attendance.

"What is there Mr Pomfret?" he exclaimed. "Is not everything to your satisfaction?"

Miss Jennings began to laugh helplessly.

"No Pascal, nothing, I'm quite all right. Tell me, who are these other people on all sides?"

The head waiter stepped back.

"Oh Mr Pomfret sir" he hissed "they are not your people, they are any peoples sir, they come here now like this, we do not know them Mr Pomfret."

"Yes Gaspard so I'd noticed" and he winked his far eye at Miss Jennings. Upon which Pascal spoke furiously to Gaspard who made off.

"For we do not see you often enough these years" Pascal said to John, bowing low to leave in his turn.

"Thank you, yes that will be all" Mr Pomfret spoke softly to the retreating back. "That man's ageless" he complained to a smiling Liz. He went on "How old would you say he was?"

"Now how about me?" she demanded.

"Oh about thirty five" he answered his own question.

"This is outrageous" Liz said. She was twenty nine.

"But it's true" John abruptly insisted. "My daughter keeps a straight face on these occasions, in fact I try Mary all sorts of times and never get a smile out of her."

"Mary's sweet" Miss Jennings announced.

"I know" her father said. "But she just hasn't that brand of humour or her nerves are over strong. Jane's Philip at twenty is the same. What is it now darling?"

"Thank God I'm too young to have children that age."

But Mr Pomfret was not it seemed to be diverted.

"If I lay in bed about to be amputated" he went on "I wouldn't expect you to laugh of course my dear and naturally Mary couldn't, but I'd lose a certain amount of resistance if I thought our acquaintances weren't roaring their beastly heads off! I'd even forgive you a grin or two" he said smiling at her.

"That's better" she said and grinned back. "You mustn't ever be serious. I can't help but laugh over the solemn way you announce these things."

"Yet you didn't break out into howls when I told about Penelope."

"That's different. I mean they make wonderful artificial feet these days." He laughed. "No" she said "I'm serious.

6

Why it might even get him out of the next war! No, with Penelope, there if you like you did something the young could never bring themselves to do."

"Don't be absurd Liz" he said equably. "You know you would tomorrow, with any little boy dressed up in a top hat and spats for a fancy dress party; in fun of course."

"But not with a girl. I'll bet Jane's Philip wouldn't! Think of having a son of twenty and a girl of six!"

"That's nothing, you're to have more than that."

"Oh I'm too old" she muttered. "No one will marry me now."

"Please Liz don't!" he protested. "In your heart of hearts you know you will."

"But I'm over twenty nine John."

"Well when you're fifty you can still have a boy of nineteen with girl of six months."

"You are sweet!" She smiled again.

"Then you do think I played Penelope a dirty trick?"

"She's a girl of course" Miss Jennings answered. "She really believed you married her so you see she thinks . . . how do I know what!"

"I still don't see it Liz."

"Oh I can't tell, I expect she may just be over-excited. Why don't you ask your Mary?"

"I daren't. She disapproves so."

"Why d'you say that about her? Oh bother children anyway! Except she isn't a child any more of course. Eighteen if she's a day. It always makes me feel old as the hills when I realise. The time I first knew you she can't have been more than twelve."

"And you look younger than she does every moment" he said smiling into Miss Jennings' eyes.

"Stop it John" she smiled back. "Mary's a very nice girl, just don't forget, and she's going to have all the young men at her heels in droves."

"Yes that's as may be. Certainly she'll have to find someone who can look after her, I shan't be able to manage much about setting up house for her husband. Who could these days? But she does disapprove. They all do."

"I expect they can't help themselves."

"Yes and why, that's what no one will tell me Liz when I ask?"

"Perhaps they want to be different from their parents."

"Poor Julia didn't laugh either" he said.

"Well if your wife never did then I suppose Mary doesn't laugh especially so as to be different to you."

"That's rather hard Liz, surely?"

"But you must have been the same with your father or mother once you'd grown up. I know I'd have done anything to be different from both mine."

"Ah children are a mystery! Just wait until you have yours."

"Haven't I already told you? It's too late, I'm too old" she wailed in a bright voice.

He reached across and laid his hand over hers on top of the white table cloth. Her nails were scarlet. He stroked the bare ring finger.

"Oh I know it's all finished between us where you're concerned but it isn't for me" she said quite cheerfully.

"Good heavens what nonsense you can talk" he replied in tones as clear as the skin of their two hands and the gold scrolls on the coffee cups. Looking up at her rather frightened nose he saw a reflection, from an empty wine glass and despatched by the sun in the Park, quiver beside her nostril.

"You're adorable" he said.

"If you only knew how I wish I were" she answered smiling.

"Oh look" he cried. "Dick Abbot's having one of his upsets with a waiter."

"Poor Jane, poor Jane" she replied, in a voice she might have used to speak of Christian martyrs and did not take her eyes from Mr Pomfret's face.

He watched Mrs Weatherby glance about with unconcern, with the especially humble half smile she used when in the same room as with what must have seemed, to her, inferior strangers, while the waiter stood relaxed beneath Abbot's purpling face. Pascal next came over in controlled haste. He stood beside this waiter, bent a little forward, eyes averted while Abbot's mouth worked and the words came tumbling out too far off for John to catch. Then Mr Pomfret stiffened and even Liz turned her head to see. Abbot was half out of the chair, was pointing a palsied finger at his adam's apple, held it there. Jane could hardly ignore this climax and laid a hand as if for reassurance on Pascal's forearm. At last Mr Abbot made gestures with slack wrists as though to brush off flies. Jane smiled again. Pascal bent forward in a torrent of humility, then chased the waiter off.

Mr Pomfret turned back to his girl friend.

"Poor old Dick! Whenever he gets upset it reminds him of that time at the club when he got stuck with a fishbone. He turned black and . . ."

"Now that's quite enough John" Miss Jennings stopped him. "In another minute you'll get me laughing and if Jane sees she'll think we're being rude."

"Well all right then" he replied in what seemed to be great good humour. "Now wait a minute, I've paid haven't I? All right then, let's go back to your great bed."

And they left, an elegant couple that attracted much attention, her sad face beaming.

"MY DEAR I'M SO SORRY" Mrs Weatherby said to her companion. Reaching across she laid a hand over his on the white table cloth. Her nails were scarlet. She gently scratched the skin by his thumbnail. Gold scrolls over white soup plates sparkled clear in the Park's sun without.

"It's nothing, only that damn waiter . . ." Mr Abbot muttered, his face alarmingly pale.

"All finished now" she assured him.

He gave a great sigh.

"Most awfully sorry" he said at last. "Can't understand what came over me."

"So blessed my dear there's still someone to speak to them these days."

"Terrible thing that half the waiters now don't know what they're serving. But I must apologise Jane. In front of John Pomfret too."

"I shouldn't let that even enter your head" she sweetly protested. Yet when he raised his dog like eyes to hers she was looking over to where John and Liz had been.

"See much of him these days?"

"Of poor John?" Her eyes came back on him. To an extraordinary degree they were kind and guileless. "Why goodness gracious me no! Not from one year's end to another."

"Can't imagine what people find in the chap."

"Oh but he has thousands of friends." She was looking round the restaurant again with her lovely apologetic smile. "Thousands!"

"Little Penelope care for the fellow?"

"Why yes how funny you should say it, now I come to think, Richard, he did come to tea only the other day, tea with her of course. He's simply sweet with darling Penelope."

"Only asked because children know you know."

She brought her eyes back once more to smile full in his great handsome face. She did not say a word.

"Because they size a man up. Instinct or something. Always prefer a child's opinion to me own."

She gave a light airy little laugh.

"And now" he went on, raising his voice, "now this damn waiter" he said and twisted right round in the chair "it's got so we'll never be served! Good God I can't apologise enough. Hardly ever see you except luncheon Sundays then this sort of thing crops up."

Pascal hastened over.

"Have you all gone home man?" Mr Abbot demanded.

"Oh sir, Mrs Weatherby madam, in two minutes, yes sir please" and Pascal went in pursuit of a head waiter.

"My dear" Mrs Weatherby smiled. "Heavens how I love this place! Why I could sit where I am this moment the whole day long."

"Decent of you" he said.

"Have you heard about Arthur Morris?" she enquired. When he shook his head she passed on what John had told.

"Good Lord" he pronounced, entirely grave. "It's serious all right then. Can't tell where these things'll stop" he added. "No telling at all! Well Jane that's bad news you bring there!"

"Isn't it dreadful" she gravely replied. "I'll have to try and see him at the clinic."

"Jolly decent if you would. To cheer the poor unfortunate fellow."

"You are sweet to be so sad" she said.

"Then John Pomfret laughed of course?"

"Well darling to tell the utter truth I couldn't help myself even. Oh, I was most to blame."

"If you did I maintain it was out of common or garden politeness, there you are. Never will understand a man like that though. Good war record, plumb through the desert, all the way up Italy, must have had umpteen fellows killed right beside him. Did he laugh then out there, – eh?"

Mrs Weatherby began to heave without a sound.

"Me being ridiculous again dear?" he asked, at his most humble.

"Only just a very little bit darling Richard. Oh I'm hopeless I know I am" she said and dabbed at her brilliant eyes with a handkerchief. "You'll have to forgive, that's all."

He watched her. His look was adoring.

"Bless you" he said.

"You are so sweet" she answered then composed herself.

Pascal and the head waiter hurried over with a trolley crowned by a dome of chromium which between them they removed with a conjurer's flourish to disclose the roast. Abbot watched this closely, leant forward to touch the plate on which they were to serve Jane's portion perhaps to make sure that it was hot and in general was threatening although at first he said very little. Mrs Weatherby, the appreciative audience, greeted this almost magical presentation with small delighted cries, praised everything but told Gaspard to take away the potatoes that he had laid, one by one, around her portion in the loving way a jeweller will lay out great garnets beside the design to which he is to work, before the setting is begun. Pascal conjured these off in what seemed to be despair.

"Sure everything's all right?" Mr Abbot demanded and put out a hand to detain Pascal in case the man had it in mind to flee.

"Simply delicious thank you. Dear Richard do start on yours. Why this is divine, simply melts in one's mouth!"

"Fetch Mrs Weatherby a sharp knife Gaspard now then" he ordered. "She can't use what she's got, man! Here give me!" He reached out a hand to Jane.

"No Richard no, you shan't. The veal's too perfect."

The trolley was withdrawn, Pascal's act over. They ate in silence for a while, appeared to be in contemplation.

"Richard" she said at last, having dabbed at her red mouth with a napkin, "I'm worried to death about my Philip!"

"What's the lad up to now?"

"Oh my dear he so needs a father's influence. The dread time has come I'm afraid! I'm fussed dear Richard."

"If I'm to help I must know more you know."

"I almost can't find the way to tell you it's all so confusing but there's Philip's whole attitude to women."

"Playing fast and loose?"

"Oh no I rather wish he would though I fear he is far too

much of a snob for that, no no, worse, it's the other, oh dear if I go on like this I never shall explain, oh but Richard what has one done to deserve things? Sometimes I almost wonder if he knows the facts of life even. You see he respects girls so!"

Mrs Weatherby made her great eyes very round and large to give Dick Abbot an adorable long glance of woe.

"Good God" he replied with caution.

"It's not often I wish his father were alive again. You remember how Jim treated me, you're my living witness darling, but oh my dear I have moments sometimes when I'm not sure what to think."

"You mean he's a . . . ?" Mr Abbot demanded lowering.

She broke into a sweet peal of laughter. "Oh Richard I do love you now and then" she cried.

"Wish you could more often" he said, rather glum.

"I'm sorry my dear, there you are. But it's a man about the house he needs I'm almost certain, an older one."

"No shortage you could marry Jane" he gruffly said. "Why there's half a dozen or more would jump at the chance."

"I couldn't dear. I'd simply never dare!"

"Why on earth not?"

"Because of darling little Penelope!!"

"But good heavens . . ."

"So jealous" she explained "such a saint I really believe she would be ill!" Her expression was of admiring love and pride.

"Are you serious?" he asked.

"You don't know what these things can be" she answered. "I'm everything to Pen, everything. She often says 'mummy I'd simply rather die'! Of course they copy the words out of one's very mouth but I'd never dare."

"Well then what is wrong with Philip?"

"He just treats girls as if they weren't real."

"How d'you want him to behave? Chuck 'em about?"

"Oh but he must learn to treat women as human beings."

"Maybe he does behind your back Jane."

She gaily laughed. "My dear I'm almost certain not" she said. "No he's so finicky with them."

"You marry again" he insisted.

"But I've got used to being alone!"

"I can believe that" he agreed. "Besides you wouldn't necessarily be doing it for yourself would you? And after all my dear we can't pay too much attention to the six-year-olds. Pen will snap out of it."

"And one thing that won't snap them out of things, as you call it, is for their poor deluded mothers to remarry."

"So you'll sacrifice Philip to little Penelope, is that the idea?"

"Richard dear one, how simply diabolically clever you can be sometimes! Oh Lord my horrid problems. But I do apologise, all this must be infinitely dull for you, and just when I'm so enjoying your delicious luncheon."

"Know what I think? I believe these things settle themselves."

"Oh but how?"

"Before you realise where you are you'll be in the Registry Office one of these days" he asserted. "And after not having asked the children's leave either."

"Do you really think I could fall in love once more?" she asked.

"I know you can" he said in a satisfied voice. She made a face.

"Richard", she grumbled and gave a scared laugh.

"Behave yourself, we were talking of marriage, not anything else, not anything!"

"Like me to have a word with him then, Jane?"

"My dear isn't that too sweet, I do appreciate it, still I very much fear he might not actually listen. Oh I realise how rude this sounds. But he's not normal! No I don't mean that. I mean more he's so old fashioned! Can you believe it he even gets up to open the door for me!! Because

14

if someone is not in the family then he never seems able to listen."

"If according to you he'll only pay attention to a step-father he'll have to wait a bit then, won't he?"

"I don't know what to do. I'm at my wit's end" she said.

"Thought you maintained you'd never remarry."

"Why Richard I never uttered a word of the kind!"

"Only man you'll get hitched onto in the end then is your faithful servant" he said with a sort of forced joviality.

"Richard dear you're quite wonderful! You can't imagine what a solid comfort you are always." She gave him an exquisitely lingering long smile.

"You wait and see" he insisted.

"I'll wait" she promised gaily laughing.

He frowned.

"Wish I could count on that" he remarked.

"My dear I do apologise" she said at once. "How abominably rude that was! But I told you I could never marry again because of little Pen. And I don't think you are being quite kind" she added with a grave reproachful look. "Richard I really believe you're almost making fun which doesn't suit you dear. Your sense of humour is not your long suit."

"I say I'm truly sorry Jane. Fact is everyone's having trouble with their children these days. Only last week John Pomfret buttonholed me in the Club about his Mary."

"I'm miserable I'm such a bore Richard." She gave him an adorable smile of humility in which there was mischief. For a moment she looked very like her daughter.

"You aren't, good Lord no" he protested.

"But I am! Anyway I think Mary's such a vulgar child."

"Flattered to find you can bring yourself to confide in me on occasions" he said at his most formal. "Never could make up my mind about her yet" he said apparently of Mary Pomfret. "Striking girl though. Why, does Philip see much of her then?"

"My Philip? Certainly not. What's John's trouble over the girl?"

"A bluestocking I fancy. Too taken up with her job. Unfeminine. Properly upset about her old John seemed."

"But how extraordinary Richard! Why that's just how I worry about Philip. So unmanly and serious for his years. What else did John say?"

"Well you know, one thing or the other."

"My dear what I do so like about you is your absolute loyalty. Of course if you'd rather not . . ."

"Tell you the truth I've pretty well forgotten now."

"In at one ear and out of the other like when I confide in you over Philip, is that it?"

"Now Jane, you know me."

"And that's just what I respect you for! It's so perfect to be sure what one pours out won't be all over London the next minute."

"Oh well" he said and seemed flattered. "But you say Philip and Mary never meet. Don't they work along the corridor in the same office?"

"Of course they do my dear. I thought everyone knew."

"Well then ask Mary what she thinks."

"But it's just because they talk every day that they don't see anything of each other. Would you take someone out at night when you sat opposite her six hours every twenty four? Really Richard what the world has come to! Besides he's too much of a snob as I said. And thank God for it where that girl's concerned!"

"Don't care for Mary then?"

"I don't see why one should be friends with one's old friends' children do you? Any more than we as children made a fuss of the horrid creatures our parents' friends brought us to play in the nursery. Of course I don't know the way Philip passes his spare time but I've a very good idea he doesn't spend that with Mary! I should hope not indeed." Mrs Weatherby began to look indignant.

"What's the gal done then Jane?"

"Nothing so far as I know, nothing at all. I couldn't care less. But just because John is one of my oldest friends I don't see why I should like his daughter even if, as you remember perfectly well, at one time I loved her mother, oh so dearly!"

There was a pause.

"Wish I knew something to suggest about Philip" he said at last.

"Let's not talk about the children any more" she said, relaxing. "Did you notice Liz and John had gone? How is that drear sad old affair of theirs have you any idea?"

"Can't imagine Jane. Don't know at all."

"I believe he's simply sick of her and she clings on in the most disgustingly squalid way." She laughed gaily again. "I can't imagine where Liz finds the strength. She's so ill!" She beamed on him. "Oh dear aren't I being ill-natured all of a sudden! You don't think I'm very wicked do you?" She leaned forward, laid her hand by his. "I tell you what" she said. "We don't want to wait for coffee here. Richard let's have it at your place darling."

His face showed eager surprise.

"I say, jolly decent of you, why not indeed? Let's go now" he said and in a few minutes they left. His great face beamed.

PHILIP WEATHERBY and Mary Pomfret were sitting in the downstairs lounge of a respectable public house off Knightsbridge.

"Will your parent ever ask a relative to the house?" he sternly enquired.

"Why no, Philip, I don't suppose he does."

"Nor my mother won't and it's inconceivable."

"I think Daddy may sometimes."

"You'd imagine my mother was ashamed of me. You see

the position? I can't ring up and say 'this is your little nephew here and can I run round for tea?'"

"Poor Philip you must come after the office one day though you'd find us rather dull for you I'm afraid."

"I'd like very much and it wouldn't be dull."

"I'll tell Daddy then."

"Have another light ale Mary?"

"Yes but this one's my turn."

"Is it? Oh all right." He took the money she had ready and went over to the bar while she got out a mirror and went over her face. In the way of the very young she did not look round the saloon.

When he came back with their drinks he said,

"D'you think our parents see much of each other still?"

"Now Philip why should they?"

"Didn't you know? They had a terrific affair once."

"But my dear how absolutely thrilling! I don't believe you."

"True as I'm here Mary. Arthur Morris told me."

"How sweet, did they really?"

"I don't think it's sweet in the least."

"I know but they had their lives to live after all. I mean their time is practically over now you see, so why shouldn't they when they chose?"

"I'm embarrassed by them that's why."

"Oh Philip are you being fair? What difference does that make?"

"We could be brother and sister for one thing."

"Only half brother. I don't mind do you?"

"Why should I?" Nevertheless he seemed quite awkward and when she looked at him out of the corner of an eye both hers creased in the tiniest amusement. "Only it's absurd that we shouldn't know" he added.

"What makes you think we might be?" she asked. He did not give a direct answer.

"D'you believe there's some special feeling between brother and sister?" he demanded.

"How about you and Penelope?"

"Oh she's too young."

"I don't suppose there can be unless they live together, – have been brought up in the same house" she corrected herself.

"You don't believe in blood?" he asked.

"Consanguinity, is there such a word?" she answered. "No more than three types surely? Daddy wore his stamped over a card he hung round his neck during the war on a ribbon he got from me. I thought that marvellous then."

"I meant heredity" he said in a severe voice.

"Oh it's all a question of environment now" she objected. "I was taught the whole question of heredity had been exploded ages back."

"All the same I'd still like to see my relatives" he complained.

"Why don't you ask your mother then?"

"She'd think it pansy. Almost told me as much once or twice."

"But you aren't Philip, no one could pretend you were."

"One never knows" he darkly answered.

"Look at you with that Bethesda Nathan at the office."

"I say, good Lord, what gossips you all are. Who says anything about Bethesda and me?" Obviously he was delighted.

"Of course we all do. Someone as attractive as you" she said smiling gently full in his face.

"You're making fun" he complained.

"No Philip don't be absurd. Naturally we gossip."

"You're laughing at me just like my mother."

"Now that's not nice and she hoots at everyone after all."

"Does she? I'd never notice."

"Every minute. It's her line" she comforted him.

"Anyway there's nothing between Bethesda and me."

"Perhaps not. What all of us are interested in is whether there may be."

"Bethesda and I discuss this entire question of relatives"

he told Mary. "She sees her own the whole time. In fact she's fed up with them."

"Jews have tremendous family feeling Philip."

"And why shouldn't they?"

"I say you are touchy! Penelope better grow up quick and take some of these awkward corners off you."

"Sorry" he said. "I'm being a bore."

"No you aren't at that" she objected. "We're having a cosy little argument that's all."

Yet what she said seemed to silence him. He turned his head away and looked round the room. She stretched her fingers out and tilted them upwards against their table, examined the short nails which were enamelled but not painted. When his eyes came upon a man with two sticks he said,

"Have you heard about Arthur Morris?"

She immediately put those hands away on her lap and smiled upon Philip.

"Who?" she asked, all charm.

"You know that great friend of both our parents."

"Oh" she said and seemed to lose interest.

"He's having his toe off."

"Whyever for?"

Both began to giggle.

"Why does a man have a toe off?" he demanded.

"How should I know?"

"Because it's diseased stupid."

"Poor man" she said no longer smiling, in an uninterested voice.

"My mother went to see him the other day" he told her.

"Well and why not? You don't make out there's something between them on top of her and Daddy?"

"I'm not sure."

"See here Philip your mother's splendid. Oh I understand she may have a slightly unmarvellous nature at least where you are concerned, but she looks wonderful!"

"What difference does that make?"

20

"All the difference. She gets so many more offers."

"But at her age it's disgusting."

"I never said she accepted them Philip. There are so many must want to take your mother out."

"Who could?"

"Don't be filthy. Much better her than I should be mauled by one of the men her age!"

"You don't mean to say that antediluvian Arthur Morris . . . ?"

"Of course not" she sharply protested. "If you go on to others like this you'll be getting me a reputation."

"I never . . ."

"OK" she said. "Forget it." She smiled. "But suppose you had to have a leg off wouldn't you wish for visitors?"

"Well of course."

"All right, then don't make out they kiss on top of the cradle they'll have put over his stump."

"Oh if it was just kissing" he said in a contemptuous voice.

"How should I know when or where they do the other?" she remarked petulantly. "I don't mind. If it's Daddy now and some woman good luck to him I say."

"Yes but your father's a man" he protested.

"I should hope so indeed" she replied at which both began to giggle again.

"You're hopeless" he said.

"I haven't half as much the matter with me as you appear to" she objected, serious once more. "Honestly you seem potty about your mother."

"I wonder if it's why the relatives won't come."

"No Philip really. You know what their whole generation is!"

"How d'you mean?"

"Well they wouldn't let a little thing like that, I mean of going to bed, what we've just been discussing, make the slightest bit of difference would they?"

"I don't believe it is a little thing."

21

"No more do I."

"That's where the whole difference lies" he said "between our generations. Their whole lot is absolutely unbridled."

"Yes Philip but they are the generation you've just said you want to meet aren't they?" Both laughed gaily at this remark.

"Damned if I can make 'em out at all" he said. "You know your father is crazy. Did you hear what he did with little Penelope the other day? When our Italian maid sent her in dressed as a bride for fun, he actually married Pen."

"Married her!"

"Pretended to of course" he explained. "Don't you think it most odd?"

"But Philip what on earth are you saying?"

"Went down on his knees in front of Mamma and from all I can make out ran through some bogus form of church service with the poor old thing. It knocked Penelope cold! She screamed the house down three days. Still she's forgetting now at last."

Miss Pomfret did not seem impressed.

"If your mother let him, then I'd say she was insane" she commented.

"Oh I don't know" he said. "But I do agree that generation's absolutely crazy."

"So are little girls, believe you me."

"And grown ones?" he enquired.

"Now to whom d'you refer may I ask?" she cried delightedly.

"Like when you went up to Derek Wolfram at the party and announced it was time for bed?"

She blushed.

"No but which beast told you?" she demanded.

"Oh that's all over the office" he announced, at which she began to giggle, he joined in and presently they left, each going their several ways with broad smiles, well content it seemed.

A FORTNIGHT OR SO LATER Mrs Weatherby was with her son Philip in the sitting room of their flat.

"Dear boy" she was saying "I'm really worried about sweet Pen this time!"

"How's that Mamma?"

"She's such a little saint."

"She always was."

"Always!" his mother fervently agreed. "But I fancy if she doesn't soon what Richard calls snap out of it then we shall just have to take her to a psychologist."

"Mr Abbot? Where does he come into things?"

"My dear" she replied. "You must not mind your mother putting her problems to old friends."

"OK Mamma. But you're about to take matters rather a long way forward surely?"

"Pen doesn't seem to get over it. Oh Philip I'm so distressed. She's just wrapped the whole thing up in her sweet mind!"

"What with? You see I don't understand."

"I never told you. I don't think one should tell one child the other's secrets. Philip I'd say it must be four weeks ago now. Oh dear doesn't time fly. John Pomfret mistakenly came to tea and Isabella so stupid of her as things turned out dressed my precious Penelope up as a real bride. Then before I could stop him he was down on his knees marrying her with the actual words out of our church service."

"Which you said over them?"

"My dear wasn't it wicked of him" she went on, ignoring her son. "And now she's desperate, yes desperate! I am so worried. I think I shall have to take her along, don't you darling?"

"But psychologists are supposed to dredge back into the past aren't they, and sister's only six?"

23

"Isn't that just what she needs Philip?"

"My point is it's only the other day."

"Yet things have already gone so very deep" she wailed. "All so hopeless! Though she doesn't say a word. She's been a little brick. I can tell though. Darling she's at breaking point!"

"How do you know Mamma?"

"How do I know? How could I tell with you when you were small?"

"You mean Penelope's really ill?"

"Sick in her mind poor little soul, perhaps even dangerously so. Oh Philip!"

"But look here Mamma . . ."

"No my dear I mean it, I've never been more serious in my life. And thank God your father isn't all over us to complicate matters."

"Well I don't see why we have to blackguard Father because we're worried about Pen."

"Don't you? I do. But I'm afraid Philip! I've got to act, rid her of this somehow."

"You put it down to the what d'you call it, the pretence?"

"I know I'm right!"

"And for that you're going to take her to a trick cyclist Mamma?"

"Don't Mamma me or use that precious slang of yours." As she said this she sweetly smiled upon him.

"Likely enough the man'll only lead her back to when she used to wet her bed" he protested.

"Philip I never thought I should have to complain of schoolboy smut in you again" she announced. "I'm surprised. It really doesn't suit you. And over your own sister please. Philip it's nasty!"

"What is?"

"The way she is taking on, the little martyr. Oh I see what there must be there deep down."

"How d'you mean?"

"Mind your own business" she replied darkly. "Pen's really suffering the sweet."

"Why after all?"

"She feels wounded. Wouldn't anyone? Oh wasn't all of it gross of him poor well-meaning John, sweet idiot of a man. For I blame myself. Oh yes I can't forget. I've had to give her sleeping draughts every night since that fated afternoon."

"Now you haven't . . ."

"Well no of course, not actually although she is just in the state I get in when I have to take them."

"I should show her to Dr Bogle."

"Dr Bogle?" she cried. "The man we go to for pills!"

"What's the use of these specialists Mamma?"

"For especial emergencies Philip. Which little girl has ever before been married at six? Tell me out of the whole history of the world!"

"Yes indeed."

"I can't understand where you get your false insensitive side my dear. She wed poor John in her own mind as sure as if she was actually in church and your father had come back from the grave to give her away, the precious! There you are. And what can you answer to that?"

"You mustn't worry" he protested.

"Then my dear she made such a picture" his mother proceeded. "In her long white veil! Somewhere she'd found a lily she was carrying, I can't imagine how unless there were some among the flowers Dick sent me. The shade of that tall lamp was askew so she stood in a shaft of light as utterly sweet as if she had been in the aisle with the sun shining through your father's memorial rose window Philip! So absurd of me my dear but the tears came to my eyes and I really couldn't see. That was the true reason why I couldn't stop it all until too late!"

"She'll recover."

"But the responsibility dear heart. You know what one

25

comes across with those awful books of Freud's I haven't read thank God."

"They're completely out of date nowadays."

"They are? You're sure? Yet there must be something in them when he's been so famous."

"He wrote about sex Mamma."

"Well isn't this sex good heavens? Sex still has something to do with marriage even nowadays hasn't it? Rising seven and to have an experience like that, I can't ever forgive myself!"

"Why not run her down to Brighton?"

Mrs Weatherby began to glow at this suggestion.

"D'you know I think I really might" she said at last. "What a brilliant idea of yours Philip, just when the weather has been so perfectly vile. Let's see, we could go tomorrow. Oh no I am meeting John. Then Sunday I was to lunch with Dick but I could put him off, that won't hurt Richard. But how will you get along dear?"

"Oh I shall be all right."

"Why not ask some girl in and have Isabella cook you one of her delicious Italian things?"

"I'll see."

"I would if I were you." Mrs Weatherby had become her old self once more. She shone on Philip the whole light of her attention. "With Chianti. Only it must be white remember. And not Bethesda please!"

When he frowned she laughed.

"Darling you mustn't mind my little teases. Don't bother. I know I'll never be told who. But one thing I am sure of. She'll be a very lucky girl."

He awkwardly smiled.

"No you must really have pity on the poor fainting souls Philip! Just imagine them sitting by their telephones bored to tears with their sad mothers who're themselves probably only dying to have an old flame in, waiting waiting to be asked, eating their lovely hearts out!"

She leant forward as though she were about to hug him.

"I might" he said.

"In a little sweat of excitement in their frocks!!" she said turning swiftly away the beautiful innocent eyes soft with what seemed to be love, her great mouth trembling.

His face showed acute embarrassment. She may have sensed this for she changed the subject.

"Do you see much of Mary Pomfret?"

"At the office" he replied.

"I can't understand someone like John having a girl like it."

He did not answer. She again went off at a tangent. "Philip what would you say if I married a second time?"

He jumped up as though he had anticipated this question, walked over to stand at the window with his back to her, a rigid back which she fixed with an apologetic look of ladylike amusement.

"It would be your own affair" he said at last, indistinctly.

"Yes I expect it could be" she replied with a small smile. "But that wasn't quite exactly what I asked. What would you say Philip?" she repeated.

"Me?" he mumbled. "Why, is there anyone?"

She laughed with great kindliness and then looked at the floor.

"Oh" she murmured "we are so queer together. You know this conversation is the wrong way round, I mean it's me should be asking you if there was someone. No of course there isn't just now for me. But suppose one day there still might? Would you find the idea so very horrid?"

He turned round. He seemed all at once to be a school-boy. She kept her face straight.

"No, I wouldn't mind" he said.

"I'd've imagined you would have liked that Philip" she went on. "Surrounded with nothing but women the whole day long, even at the office from all I can make out."

"Honest" he said "don't bother about me. I'm OK. It wouldn't make a bit of difference." He smiled.

"These things do happen" she murmured reproachfully.

27

"Not putting up the banns then?"

"Don't be so silly dear!"

"Who's it to be Mamma?"

"No but really I shall be quite cross with you in a minute. There's no one. But your mother's not so long in the tooth yet that it mightn't come about. Philip wouldn't you a little bit like to have a stepfather?"

"I don't think you'd marry again just to give me one."

"My dear how sharp you are sometimes" she laughed. "You got me there all right or did you? Not that I don't think of you and you of me, you are simply sweet to me always, bless your heart."

"Well let me know when and I'll put the wedding march on the record changer. I say look at the time. I must be off."

"Good heavens yes" she cried "and I've stockings and shoes to get for our little nervous case, the martyr."

At this she went up to Philip, kissed him with fervour and they both left.

AT THE SAME TIME on the identical day Mary Pomfret sat with her father in their living room.

"What would you say if your devoted parent married a second time?" he asked.

"Oh Daddy how thrilling for you. Who?"

"I don't know wonderful, I was only wondering."

"Are you sure?"

"You seem very certain someone would agree."

"Of course!"

"And you wouldn't mind?"

"But is it Miss Jennings?"

28

"Now wait a minute Mary. I wasn't even making up my mind to ask anyone. Mine is just an idle question."

"Well are you very discontented as you are then Daddy?"

"What do you mean by that?"

"I can't see why any man ever marries his girl" she said. He laughed.

"You're dead right" he answered. "It often comes as a great surprise."

"Not to the man; he has to ask."

"To both" he insisted. She considered this. Then she said, "Why did you want to know whether I minded?"

"Surely nothing could be more natural dear? Of course I'd have to know first."

"Don't I still look after you and the flat all right then?"

"But you are perfect, absolutely perfect."

"I thought perhaps you might wish for a change." Her face expressed embarrassment. He yawned.

"My dear" he said gently "one doesn't remarry to get a change of housekeeping. Not yet at all events."

"That's what will happen when that happens in case you don't realise."

"Oh Mary no. Not at my age!"

"But of course I'd have to go" she said in a distressed tone of voice. "I couldn't stay to witness you and your bride."

"My dear" he objected "it would not be so romantic and after all there's room in plenty in the flat for three people."

Her blue eyes filled with tears she was so young.

"Liz wouldn't like it" she insisted.

"Now Mary" he said and seemed alarmed "I told you there was no one. I just thought I'd ask to get your reactions. Good Lord you'll be going off one day and wouldn't expect me to stay on here alone."

"I don't see why not. I mean you can invite in anyone you want can't you?"

"I could be lonely" he explained with what appeared to be a false voice as he selected a cigarette.

"I'm always here now" she said.

"But you ought to go out more Mary."

"How shall I when nobody asks me."

"They will. I say let's give an entertainment. Why not? Lots of young men for you and hang the expense!"

"Oh I shan't want anyone."

"Nonsense, that's because you don't know them. You leave it to me darling."

"No honestly, you have your own friends in if you're dull."

"Who says I'm dull?"

"Well you've just explained that you'll re-marry, haven't you Daddy?"

"But good Lord one doesn't go through all that again simply because one's dull."

"Don't you?"

"No" he said, reached up a hand to where she stood by his chair and pulled her down to kiss an ear. She sat on the arm.

"Anyway I never shall" she laughed.

"You will" he said. They lapsed into easy silence.

"It's dark. Wouldn't you like me to put the light on?" she asked.

"No. Let's save money for our party. This fiendish rain!" he commented.

"You must miss your mother?" he said at last. He asked the question once a year and each time got a different answer. On this occasion she replied,

"I don't know. I can't remember her."

"It must be very dull for you here alone with me."

She ignored this. "Who was her best woman friend?" she murmured.

"Jane."

"Mrs Weatherby?" she exclaimed in great surprise. "You never told."

"Oh they were always together" he assured his daughter.

He laughed. "Never out of each other's pockets at one time."

"I had no idea, not in the least. Well that does make a bit of difference!"

"How d'you mean darling?"

"I'll look at her quite differently" Miss Pomfret said in an altered voice.

"She's very nice" her father assured her.

"You aren't thinking of marrying Mrs Weatherby then Daddy?"

"Now listen, I told you didn't I? There's not a soul, there really isn't. I'm sorry I spoke. It was just a stupid thing one says glibly, then regrets."

"But marriage might be right for you."

"There isn't time" he wailed in his affected voice. He twisted round to smile on her face. "All this work! We none of us have the leisure to wed! It's too frightful!"

"Oh by the way, talking of her" she mumbled "I told Philip to come round to tea."

"Not Saturday!"

She frowned. "No, no" she said. "But he seems rather blue at home."

Mr Pomfret opened wide eyes. He had a question wandering round his mouth. But he shut his lips. Then he asked with indifference,

"How's little Pen?"

"Oh she's all right. She's just spoiled" the daughter said. "Why did you never tell me about Mrs Weatherby Daddy?"

"What about her?"

"That she was Mummy's best friend."

"Oh I must have often" he yawned.

"No. Never before. And I wonder why?"

"Well I don't say often enough what a wonder you are do I? I suppose the obvious soon gets forgotten. I forgot you didn't know and in case I forget again I'll say this once more, you're wonderful love and no man could have a nicer daughter." He yawned again.

It was too dark to see the expression on her face.

"Don't get all woolly stupid" was what she replied. There was a pause.

"How's the job going?" he drowsily enquired.

"Oh much the same."

"Still scissors and paste?"

"Some of the girls have gone out and bought their own to cut with" she answered. "The ones they issue now are quite hopeless. Yes we snip bits out of the newspapers, stick them on folio sheets, and it's still all cabled out to Japan where the press people hardly use any of what we send. It'll go on like that for ever."

"See much of Philip?" His voice came even lower. She looked down but could make out no more than the dark top of his head. She glanced up at the framed reproductions and in this light they were no more than blurs.

"See him?" she murmured.

"What's that?" he mumbled.

"He's in C Department" she softly answered, beginning to space out the words, stroking his hair so the tips of her fingers barely touched his head. "In C Department" she repeated even softer, as if to sing them both to sleep. "But yes I see him. Sometimes" she whispered. "Sometimes but not often." A small silence fell. "Not often" she went on at last so low she could hardly be heard. Her father began to snore. "But I do sometimes" she ended almost under her breath, got up and left him slumbering.

THE NEXT DAY was Sunday. John Pomfret sat over luncheon at the usual table looking out on the Park, with Miss Jennings.

"So I asked her right out" he was saying in his pleasantly

affected party manner, "I said 'would it matter to you if I married again?'"

Miss Jennings appeared to listen with care.

"Oh Liz" he cried and spread his arms out over two dirty plates on which were soiled knives and forks, two glasses of red wine, and a bottle in its gay straw jacket, "she made a picture, you know she's a remarkable girl. Mary stood there like an angel, just a Botticelli angel framed in my lovely Matisse over the fireplace, those lozenges of colour perfect as a background for that pretty head. When I think how she's carried on for years without a woman to talk with I feel ashamed and proud Liz!"

"What did Mary say then?"

A faint shade of embarrassment seemed to come over his handsome features.

"Not much" he replied.

"How d'you mean?" she anxiously asked.

"No man could be luckier in a daughter" he said. "Not one moment of worry, nary one. Of course if Jane hadn't quarrelled with Julia before she died I might easily have called on Jane for help. I know I thought of it. But Liz it seemed disloyal to my wife, she would have turned in her poor grave. So I struggle on alone."

He paused. Miss Jennings appeared incapable of speech. He was gazing through the great window on what looked to be a white sheet of water from which a few black trees in bud leaned against driving rain.

"And it's come out quite perfect" he proceeded. Miss Jennings blinked. "I can't say too much in praise of my girl. So I'm going to give a party!"

"A party?" she exclaimed.

"Well she doesn't meet enough people" Mr Pomfret announced. "How could the child when she looks after me at night and works all day? I'm not much use to her Liz" he said. "My wretched job keeps me pretty well occupied! But Mary never gets a minute off."

33

"That makes two in that case."

"How d'you mean?" he enquired.

"There's Jane going to give a twenty firster for Philip and now you'll have yours."

"I never heard about Philip's" he protested. "As a matter of fact I was to have had drinks yesterday at Jane's but she went off to Brighton with Penelope and Dick Abbot. Jane would have told me then only she never got the chance. Who's she having?"

"Oh all of us I believe John."

"And some young people too I should hope" he said. "So dreadful dull with nothing but us older ones."

"Speak for yourself" she protested rather drily.

"I was" he assured her. "In that case I think I shall wait until I see how Jane's comes off. I really can't afford a party, who can these days! Yes I'd rather wait and see. Of course Mary and I will be invited."

"Did you think of giving a dance with champagne?"

"My dear girl where's the money to spring from? And you can't make out it's expected nowadays!"

"People do. Several get together still" she explained.

"No that wouldn't go at all" he decided. "Only yesterday bless her I asked if there were even anyone Mary specially wanted and she wouldn't have it. No let's see what sort and kind of a show Jane puts on first."

"And how's little Penelope?" she enquired.

"My dear Liz damn all that silly nonsense is what I insist. The child's just living till she can pick on something new to upset her, you mark my words."

"I'd've thought it made everything so difficult with Jane."

"Old Jane's all right" he said. "But my God you're lucky not to have children of your own yet Liz."

"I wouldn't mind" she muttered.

"Well I must say that's a weight off me now I haven't to give a do for Mary right off" he announced, visibly taking heart. "Yes you're lucky all right. Lord the things that keep coming up! No rest at all. Though I've not got anything against the child, please understand."

"Mary's sweet" she agreed in a perplexed voice.

He thought of something else.

"How did you come to hear of Jane's party?" he demanded.

"Philip told me."

"I didn't know you ever saw him" Mr Pomfret complained with lazy amazement.

"I had to go round to the office. As a matter of fact my business took me to his boss" she boasted.

"So did you look in on Mary in M?"

"There wasn't time darling and I'm not sure she'd have been overjoyed."

"Good God Liz what nonsense you can talk. Why Mary'd have loved it! Pity you didn't you know. She's managing marvellously well. No more than a junior in length of service of course but already she's established and doing damned important work too let me tell you. To tell the truth I once knew her chief. I'm always meaning to ring the woman one day to ask. But what holds me back is Mary's face if she got to hear. Oh she's independent Liz, and won't take any manner or means help. And I respect her for it."

"Philip was handing round the tea and buns" Miss Jennings informed him. He burst into laughter.

"Well maybe my dear you did best not to explore further than Department C. You might have come on Mary with a mop and bucket between M and N. No, as for her it's not only what she tells me, which is little enough in all conscience, because I have other sources, I know what I'm talking about. But I'm not far wrong when I say Philip's an ungodly failure. What you told me just now doesn't come one bit as a surprise."

"Is that really so? I had no idea" Miss Jennings protested and seemed pleased.

"Don't breathe a word to anyone least of all to Jane" he

35

implored. "He's not quite all she's got, there's still little Penelope practising to become St Francis, but it would kill poor Jane all the same. Oh now what made me say any of that! Liz I'm growing crabbed and ill-natured in middle age."

"You aren't" she said.

"I jolly well am! Oh yes, worse luck! Never mind. Forget it."

"Good heavens John you remember about nine weeks ago when we were discussing his mother and she promptly came in, well here's Mary with Philip."

He twisted round in the chair.

"They can't afford this" he said into the room in a loud voice. Then he saw. They were standing before Pascal, close together in an attitude of humility while the man sneered in their faces. It was plain they were not known.

"Excuse me Liz" Mr Pomfret asked over a shoulder. He got up. "Can't have that you understand" he said and went across. "Hello there" he called. Pascal and Gaspard stepped back as he strode to kiss Mary. She seemed to shrink while Philip put on an embarrassed grin. Mr Pomfret shook him warmly by the hand. After some more talk which Miss Jennings watched with a tender smile, Pascal, obsequious again, at once led the young couple away to a good table. As they went John said something to his daughter who sent Liz a startled glance.

When he sat down once more John said "Well I only hope he pays."

Miss Jennings replied "why here she comes."

Mr Pomfret rose to his feet. "Fancy seeing you" Mary greeted Miss Jennings shyly. Her wrist was loose when she took Miss Jennings' hand.

"Oh darling" Liz cried "you look so sweet."

"You both do look wonderful" Mary mumbled. Another phrase or two and she made her escape. As he sat down again the father said with satisfaction,

"My girl's got manners. I rather pride myself on that as a matter of fact."

"She's sweet" Miss Jennings repeated. "You didn't expect to see them here then?"

"Those two? My dear Liz I never interfere. But I certainly imagined she was lunching back home this afternoon. Not that she can't do just as she likes of course. I thought she said something about tea. I must have misheard. And I didn't know they ever met."

There was a pause while he watched his daughter.

"Were you told about Arthur Morris?" she next enquired.

"No? Not more bad news, you can't surely mean? What is it?" he asked turning back to her.

"Now they're having to take the ankle off."

This time neither laughed or even smiled.

"Good Lord" he cried "like so much else it's beginning to be a bad dream. Who's his doctor then? Can't they do anything for him?"

"Poor Arthur isn't it bad luck?" she said.

"Frightful" he agreed. "Now what are you proposing to have now? Cheese or sweet or both? Where is Gaspard? First they don't or won't recognise one's own children and then they can't bother to take an order. Here Pascal!" He waved.

"Only coffee for me darling. I must watch my figure."

"Would you mind if I had just a bite of cheese? Look Pascal you won't give my daughter a table and then there's no one to get us on with Miss Jennings' luncheon! She'd simply like some white coffee and I'll have cheese and biscuits."

The man hurried off. "What were we saying?"

"About Arthur."

"Why" he protested "it's the most frightful thing I ever heard in all my life! Poor old fellow. No knowing where these things'll stop either. And the bill too if you don't mind, waiter. I am sorry to hear that" he ended.

"It's when a man must wish he'd married" Miss Jennings said reflectively. "Having a leg off."

"Never forget William Smith" he objected.

"William Smith?" she echoed. "I don't remember."

"Perhaps he was a bit before your time. He got into a motor smash, lost both arms and Myra left him."

"Was he married?"

"But I've just told you! Yes Myra went. And she got her decree on incompatibility of temperament."

"Perhaps that had been going on a long time John."

"It's very dangerous to lose a limb when you're married" he announced. "Two limbs are almost always fatal. So watch out."

"Oh I wouldn't think much of a husband who left as soon as I happened to be maimed" she cried.

"The thing is they do. And damn quick too! Without even a by your leave!"

"No John that's dreadful!"

He let out a great gay laugh.

"It's the way of the world" he explained. "Anyway lucky old Arthur isn't married is he?"

"No, but all the same!"

"Forget it I was only joking" he said.

There was a pause while he fondly smiled and she seemed lost in thought.

"Will she ask me?" she enquired at last.

"Who darling?"

"Jane of course."

"What to? I can't tell how you mean?" he objected.

"This party she's to give so you can make up your mind whether you'll have one after."

"Naturally she will."

"Why darling?" she wanted to know.

"She'd better" he announced.

"I don't fancy Jane likes me" Miss Jennings insinuated.

"Ask us without each other?" he protested. "That would be unheard of, dear."

"Have the invitations gone out already John?"

"But most certainly not. Jane doesn't even realise she's giving a party yet, not before she and I have talked it over. And she can't if she won't ask you."

"John you're being very sweet yet I wonder if Jane really likes me?"

"She loves you" he roared.

"No, that's going too far" she insisted. "You spoil it!"

"You don't understand" he said. "She depends on you. She knows very well I wouldn't come if you weren't there and Jane relies on me."

"And so what do you mean by that, darling?"

"Precisely the little I'm saying. Since her husband died she's never given anything without she had all her old men friends round her, she wouldn't dare."

"You say she'll invite me only because of you."

"That's so."

"Well then it's not very nice is it?"

"Liz darling you're trying to trap me. She adores you."

"Does she? I don't think I'll come then."

"Look darling" he said "with this frightful rain this is not one of those days we can take our customary Sunday walk." He laughed. "Come Liz" he said "let's get back to bed."

"Aren't you awful! Oh! I suppose so, all right" she replied, getting up to go at once, giving a shy smile.

MISS POMFRET WAVED to her father as he left with Miss Jennings while Philip made as if to rise from his place. When he had settled down again he said,

"Have you heard about this party my mother's to give?"

"Oh Philip but when? And are you inviting me?"

"Of course."

"How kind! Oh dear how nice." She beamed upon him. "When is it?"

"There'll be weeks of talk yet. While she makes up her mind how not to ask a single one of our relations. No at the moment it's to be for my friends, only she knows quite well I haven't any."

"Surely that's nonsense Philip. What about the men you knew at school?"

"I've lost touch."

"Well it wasn't so long ago after all?"

"They none of them work in London" he said in a severe voice as though to discourage questions. "I don't know where they are now. But she accuses me of behaving as apparently I used to when she came down to my first school."

"You'll have to tell me a little more if I'm to understand" Miss Pomfret gently said.

"She was always in the car" he explained. "When we passed any of the other chaps I used to duck right down just as if" and here he copied his mother's emphatic speech "'just as if they had guns, repeating rifles.'"

"And did you?"

"Of course we every one of us did. You don't spend entire weeks with the creatures only to want to see them when you can get away for an hour or so. Besides there was too much chromium plate on the beastly thing. It was vulgar."

"Oh no Philip."

"Were you at school?"

"As a matter of fact I wasn't."

"And I suppose at a girls' establishment you did anything you could to show off?"

"I expect they did" she meekly replied.

"I used to see the girls out with their parents in hotels Mamma took me to tea" he muttered. "But the point, no, part of the point is that Mamma as she accused me of trying to duck every time we passed anyone, suited her action to the words or whatever the phrase may be and bumped her head down on the sofa she was sitting in to show me how I used to behave and smashed one of her eyebrows against a heavy glass ashtray she'd put beside herself." He laughed.

"Did she hurt her forehead?" Miss Pomfret enquired warily.

"Just a bump" he answered. "Sometimes Mamma is rather wonderful." He was smiling. "She's so violent."

"I think your mother's sweet now, Philip!"

"Well the fact is, when she hurt herself it set her off and I got the whole thing again all over. How even at Eton I hadn't any friends, still never saw a soul these days, what was I doing with my life, all that sort of usual trouble. And lastly of course she wanted to know, would she have to have all over again the whole of this wretched experience that had made her so miserably unhappy with little Penelope when Pen grows up."

"Oh but Philip you aren't really making your mother unhappy are you?"

"It's just the way she speaks you understand. Why, are you the joy of your father's life at the moment?"

She laughed. "I really believe I am" she replied. "How is your kid sister anyway?"

"As well as can be expected. For the time being there's nothing on her mind of course. But even at Eton we didn't want to see each other either. It was torture going to the theatre the night before one went back, there were so many. They even sat right next."

"You mean you simply couldn't bear to see them again now?"

"Oh no" he protested. "Of course it's quite different now. I just don't want to see any of 'em that's all."

"Well then you needn't."

"The only thing is" he said in a rueful way "I'm supposed to have this party for my twenty firster."

"But Philip" she cried "in that case you can't not invite your friends."

41

"You know what it is with Mamma. The ones she does eventually ask will all come out of her set inevitably in the end. They won't be contemporaries of mine."

"I could rake up a few girls" she volunteered.

"I don't mean anything against her" he said, seeming to ignore Mary's offer. "I've known this happen before. And of course when Penelope's little time comes there'll be thousands of young men Mamma will have in, all that part of it is in my mother's blood. No, but where I am concerned, she's making an excuse to throw a party of her own. Apart from which one has to be sorry for parents. They had such a lot of money once and we've never seen what that was."

"I think it's a shame" she said rather mysteriously.

"If she wants to give her own 'do' why shouldn't she? And my twenty firster provides the excuse because I know she can't afford two."

"But you should have your friends in for your own twenty firster Philip."

"You don't understand" he said. "If I told her that, she's incredibly generous and she'd lend me the flat for the evening and enough money to give another."

"Then why don't you?"

"Because we can't afford it."

"I believe you simply won't bother with a party of your own Philip."

He laughed.

"Well" she said "it's your life after all."

"But I do wish she'd ask the relations" he insisted.

"Who've you got specially in mind?" she demanded.

"Uncle Ned" he replied then rather mysteriously paused.

"What's so thrilling about him?" she asked.

"I see you haven't got the idea" he said. "I imagine you either have the feeling or you don't. I just feel a thing for my family that's all. Oh we're nobodies, our names have never been in history or any of that rot, I simply'd like to see them and I don't ever seem to."

"You can when you're married."

42

"How d'you mean?"

"It was what you said the other day Philip about not liking to ring your relations to propose yourself to tea. Well once you marry a girl you'll be able to ask your uncle round as often as you please for him to get to know her."

"That's quite an idea" he agreed.

She watched him with an unfathomable expression.

"It's a bit stiff though to have to marry to meet one's uncle" he protested at last.

"Nothing's easy" she said. "Oh nothing's ever easy" she repeated. A pinched look came over her face. She pushed her empty plate away. "You get fed up" she muttered. "Sick of it all!"

"Why whatever's the matter?"

"I don't know" she said and looked as if about to cry.

"I say I'm most dreadfully sorry. Would you like to go outside or something."

"Everything's so hopeless" she announced in a low voice.

"Are you all right?" he asked.

She appeared to pull herself a little together.

"I don't seem to get anywhere with my life Philip" she said not looking at him, eyes averted. "I mean" she went on and began to speak louder, with some assurance "I mean now that the only jobs one can land, or the only ones within my reach, are State jobs, well I just can't move on, get promotion, arrive at the top where there's just the one person, you know. In the days there was more private industry one could change around but as I am, I'm no more than in a Grade which I drag about with me like a ball and chain if I apply for another Department."

"You wouldn't want to go back to the bad old times Mary" he gently remonstrated. "Not when we're making this country a place fit to live in at last."

"A ball and chain dragging at one all the time" she echoed as if she had not heard him. "And so it will be the whole of my life. I'll do a little bit better every year and get nowhere in the end."

"Mary" he cried "you're discouraged!"

"You're telling me?" she asked, showing signs of indignation.

"No but look at all the way we've come the past few years" he protested.

"Oh yes" she agreed in an uninterested voice.

"And we're not working for ourselves now" he went on. "At least not those of us who are worth anything, like you and me. Besides, if you'll forgive my being personal, you'll marry, have children."

"Will I?" she said in a small voice.

"Of course you must" he announced with what was almost impudent assurance.

"I don't think I shall Philip. But suppose I do, what will happen to them? Are they to work through a few Grades until they reach retiring age by which time I'll be dead?"

"There's your grandchildren" he said not so confidently.

"How d'you know?" she demanded in a loud scornful tone then bit her lip.

There was a pause while he crumbled bread into pellets. He looked at her again. The face he saw seemed even younger, wore an expression of childish obstinacy.

"You were talking of my party" he tried. "Why don't you persuade your father to have one for you?"

"Oh Philip" she protested and gave him a hard, angry look "one dance doesn't alter everything for ever does it!"

"I know" he said at last "I get moments of utter discouragement too."

"You do Philip?" Her voice was softer.

"Fifty two weeks in the year and we work fifty" he muttered.

"And they say buy a new hat so you'll feel different" she agreed.

"But we've got everything before us haven't we?" he moaned as if he were looking down into his own grave.

"Year in year out" she assented.

"Sometimes it seems hopeless" he said and in his turn

took on an appearance of obstinacy younger even than his years. As she watched him she visibly brightened.

"Cheer up Philip" she encouraged. "Things may not be as bad for all that."

"Here" he demanded, obviously puzzled. "I thought you were the one who saw no hope."

"Oh come on" she cried. "Let's not sit here any more, glooming Sunday afternoon away! What about a film?"

"I'd love to if you would" Mr Weatherby replied, back at his most formal, and in a short time they were off past the small round tables, with older people glancing up at them. As a couple they kept themselves to themselves under scrutiny, and would probably appear bright and efficient to their elders, quite a mirror to youth and the age they lived in.

They hardly spoke again that day, a kind of blissful silence lay between.

THE FOLLOWING MORNING, on the Monday, Mary Pomfret rang up her office to say she was indisposed and took a train to Brighton. Philip did the same. Neither knew what the other had done and they did not see one another on the way down.

Mary went straight to Mrs Weatherby's hotel but Philip strode off in the opposite direction. Soon he came to a pewter sea on which a tramp steamer was pushing its black smoke out in front and he had to lean himself against wind and rain.

Miss Pomfret selected a chair in full view of the lift and not long afterwards when Mrs Weatherby descended she waved, went up to the gates to greet Jane. This lady seemed disconcerted.

45

"My dear" she said "am I supposed to recognise you?"

"Why how do you mean?"

"Are you alone Mary?"

Miss Pomfret laughed and appeared embarrassed.

"I think I must be" she said. "I don't see anyone else."

"My dear you will forgive, you really must, but it was such a queer surprise. No, not so very long ago one never was sure whether to go up to a friend in this wretched uncomfortable place. You see there was no knowing if they wanted to be known. Absurd but there it is."

"Well I did rather need to see you as a matter of fact."

"You darling, then it's a visit" Mrs Weatherby cried although she still seemed wary and once or twice looked over a shoulder. "Come, where shall we choose for a cosy talk. But what a long way to travel" and chattering as if delighted she led the girl to a corner from which she could not be observed by anyone passing through the main lounge.

"I was killing two birds with one stone I suppose actually" Miss Pomfret explained with obvious discomfort. "Oh no, such a rude way to put it! As a matter of fact there was something I simply had to ask. Something that came up the other day when I talked to Daddy."

The older woman seemed to pay a great deal of attention to the exact positioning of the diamond clip in the V of her dress.

"You see he said something about my mother" Mary went on. "And you" she added.

Mrs Weatherby sat up very straight.

"It's too wicked the wicked tongues there are" she cried in great indignation and at once. "I only hope my dear you won't ever have some such terrible experience you can look back on in your life and be sure that all your poor ills date right from it. Oh I went to my lawyer but he said let sleeping dogs lie, don't stir up mud, better not throw glass stones. I don't know if I did right, yet oh they should have been punished!"

46

"Please I didn't realise, I'm so sorry" Miss Pomfret murmured. "What can it have been?"

"I couldn't possibly tell" Jane protested. "I'd rather bite my own tongue off first. And so deceitful" she wailed. "People I'd known all my life, thought were my best friends!"

"By the way don't tell Philip I came" Mary interposed at her most ill assured and nervous.

Mrs Weatherby at once assumed a mantle of tragic calm and decision.

"Then you know everything" she proclaimed in a low voice.

The two women stared at each other in amazement. Suddenly Jane laughed. A good-natured smile spread across her face but there was still a trace of slyness about the eyes. Miss Pomfret looked small, frightened, and bewildered.

"Then what exactly did dear John say?" the elder asked with a casual tone of voice.

"Only that Mummy and you were great friends."

"Darling Julia" Mrs Weatherby assented. "And you are so like her dear. Simply the living spit! I am very fond of John" she added then waited rather out of breath.

"You see I've never had anyone tell me about Mummy" the girl said with an appealing smile.

"But doesn't dear John?"

"Oh you know what Daddy is."

"Yes I see, I see. What was it exactly you wanted to find out?"

"But everything, how she was like, everything."

"Of course. Look my angel" Mrs Weatherby beamed on Mary "I'm such a stupid, so you will forget all I said about idle tongues won't you? I thought" she went on obviously at random "you'd heard something about that absurd houseparty. It was in Essex before you were born. But simply invented, every single word made up! I suppose people had much more time on their hands those days which made them so dangerous. Darling Julia!!" She sighed.

"Darling darling Julia and how she would have simply been overjoyed to be sitting looking at you here this instant minute!"

There was pause during which Jane gazed earnestly into Miss Pomfret's face.

"Did you go down to stay in Essex together then in those days?" the girl enquired at last.

"Never once" Mrs Weatherby replied immediately. "Put all that right out of your sweet mind. Now promise me. You see my dear you were a little sudden, weren't you, so lovely there by the lift! And I was just a tiny bit upset."

"Why, is anything wrong?"

Jane gave the girl a shrewd look.

"These beastly servants" she said. "Half the time they don't know the dish they're serving. But how selfish of me! What was it you wanted about your dear mother?"

"I'm so ashamed" Mary excused herself. "Suddenly turning up like this of course you wouldn't understand at first."

"But where did you learn how to find me? You are really clever and so sweet with it."

"Philip said." At this Mrs Weatherby started. "Why that wasn't anything awful was it."

"Awful?" Mrs Weatherby echoed, her response to this colder. At that moment Richard Abbot appeared for a minute on the way out behind his bags but Miss Pomfret had her back towards him. "Awful?" Jane repeated. "Good gracious me I should hope not. No it's just that little Penelope is ever such a little bit run down and I always think the wind down here is splendid don't you for all that sort of thing. No we've been like mice" she added "like mice, just breathing the air in. We simply haven't seen a soul."

"She got upset didn't she playing at being married?"

Mrs Weatherby took this with great good humour.

"Well my dear" she said "I can at least tell who you got that from. Oh no I'm not blaming, Philip is so sweet with his sister only dear Mary I can speak out to you can't I, but sometimes he does rather overdo things don't you think, makes them to be more than they really are. It's true an old friend came to tea and Penelope dear darling was a wee bit upset after." Mrs Weatherby paused, seemed to reflect. "She's so sensitive and jealous. It was one of my dearest friends, we went to dances together, had all the same partners, I've known her for years. And you know how things are. Soon as you have children of your own you'll come upon this very same problem you sweet soul! When they're brought in after tea they expect undivided attention, the wonderful pets, and I suppose Pen thought she was being a trifle neglected."

"Probably mine will be at my skirts all day long if I have any" Miss Pomfret commented shyly. "But did this friend know Mummy too?" she asked.

"We all loved Julia" Mrs Weatherby answered. "Why we loved her!"

"Did you know Daddy too then?"

"Of course you angel! It was almost a double wedding. We were never a moment out of each other's houses at one time. Your beloved mother was my dearest friend!"

"Who did you get to love first?"

There was a pause then Jane cried,

"Just listen to you. Isn't that sweet!" And Mrs Weatherby's extraordinary eyes did at this moment fill with tears. So she went on for twenty minutes about Julia's perfections following which, after hardly putting another question, Mary excused herself and left.

Once she was outside the girl hurried back to the station.

Mrs Weatherby had just set her face to rights when she looked up to find her son Philip standing there.

"Good Lord dear boy have you seen Mary?" she cried.

"I had lunch with her yesterday" he said.

"No just now not an instant ago" she insisted.

"My sweet Mamma she's in the office cutting out an article on English cherry blossom for the Japanese."

"What are you down here for then?"

49

"Oh I thought I'd have a change. To tell the truth I'd something I rather wanted to ask."

"And you came all the way down to Brighton just for that?"

"It wasn't anything I could mention over the phone. Look here you won't be annoyed will you but am I Father's son?"

Mrs Weatherby went deep red under the make-up.

"Are you what?" she demanded menacingly.

"All right Mamma forget this" he said in haste.

"What has one done to deserve it?" she claimed in a low voice. She looked closely at his hangdog face. Then she again began to laugh. "Oh God" she said. "Forgive me dearest but what a gowk you are! So you're in love with her isn't that the thing? Or is it more of this damned snobbery? Philip do take your hat off and sit down. You can't stand in a hotel lobby to ask questions like you just have of your very own mother your flesh and blood and remain covered!" He sat at her side. "There" she said "that's better. Are you sure you feel quite all right? Are you contemplating marriage Philip?"

He mumbled no.

"Quite sure?" she asked. "So this is the reason she wished to see me then" she added.

"Who?"

"Mary."

"No Mamma what can she have wanted? You say she's been here?"

"Why all the hurry though dear boy? Good God but you aren't now proposing to elope? With Mary? Oh my dear." She peered at him with her marvellous soft eyes as though he might be ill. "Please oh please don't do anything sudden darling, always such a mistake" she said. She laid a white fat hand on his forearm to restrain him. "If much happened I'd never be able to look poor John in the face after" she appealed. "Promise me! But you're wet" she cried "you're soaked through." She moved her hand to his forehead. "It's burning!" she announced. "That's how it is then, you're in a high fever, don't know what you're doing, oh dear and in a hotel too. Did you see little Penelope?"

"Who Mamma?"

"I'm so worried but this of course explains everything, you've a great temperature. No I've been fussed about the darling if you really want an answer to your stupid question. There are some people here who seemed perfect and I let her run out with their child, the two of them are just of an age. Now look my dear boy you must change at once and have a good hot bath. No arguments please. Oh you'll be the death of me with your pneumonia and your silly insane ideas! Here's the key to my room. Have a really hot bath and sit in my dressing gown while I see the manager."

"See the manager?" he echoed.

"To get your clothes dried of course" she told him. "You don't suppose I specially bring a change of suits for you when I come away for the weekend and haven't been told that you're to pay me a visit unannounced. If children only knew the worry and responsibility they are to parents."

"But I'm all right" he protested.

"You sit there and say that to my face after all you've just asked about me; no I don't want to worry you but you're seriously ill Philip or it would be better for you if you were! Perhaps though in spite of everything you're just insane."

He sat apparently unmoved.

"I'm sorry, I do apologise" he said.

"You'll forgive me but your whole generation's hopeless I must say it, so there!" Mrs Weatherby pronounced, still in the low tones she had used all along to voice her indignation. "You're prudes, there's this and that can't be discussed before you and then you come out with some disgusting nonsense of which you should be thoroughly ashamed. I'm in despair that's all, I'm simply in despair!"

"I had to know" he said.

"That's quite enough" she cried. "Now be off at once

and have your bath or I shall be quite cross. No do go Philip
or you'll catch your death."

He went. She settled back like a great peacock after a dust
bath, sighing.

WHEN MISS POMFRET got back to London she rang
Arthur Morris to ask if it would be convenient to call. She
arranged to have tea with him at the nursing home.

"This is really nice of you Mary" he said as she came in.
"Just what your mother would have done. Julia was the
kindest woman in the world."

Miss Pomfret seemed at her brightest.

"Was she? Did you know her well?" she asked, making
the question into flattery.

"You see we were all in the one set, went about together,
stayed great pals most of the time."

"Most of the time?" she echoed with an artless
expression.

"Well it must be so with your generation" Mr Morris
answered. "We had our ups and downs. People fall out then
come together again. Don't you find that?"

"Me? Oh I haven't any friends."

"Haven't any friends, a pretty girl like you? Or is there
something wrong?"

"Wrong with me!" she cried.

"So you see you've got hundreds of 'em" he concluded.

"I haven't, honestly. I don't think we meet the number
of different people you used to."

"It may not be quite the same for girls of course but boys
still go to Eton don't they?"

"I suppose" she said. "Did Mummy know many?"

"Etonians?"

"Don't be idiotic" she demanded smiling. "No, people of course."

"Yes" he said "a beautiful woman like that would have, wouldn't she?"

"And Mrs Weatherby and she got married at the same time?"

"They did" he replied.

"D'you think Philip and I look like each other?" she asked.

"No I don't."

"Who were her other friends?"

"Your mother? Well everyone of our lot. You've seen 'em about again and again whenever your father invites them in."

"He's to give another party now" she announced.

"Don't tell me that just when I'm stuck here like this!"

"But you'll be out soon?"

"Oh I expect so. When is it?"

"This is funny" she said. "You know how cautious Daddy can be. It seems Mrs Weatherby's planning one and he wants to see how hers goes before he commits himself."

"I don't know why he need" Mr Morris objected. He hitched himself back against the pillows as though the cradle under bedclothes over his leg were sucking his whole body towards the foot. "They'll be the same old crowd in the end" he added.

"And was that the case when Mummy was alive?"

"How d'you mean?"

"Well anyway who were her particular friends?"

"We've all kept together, those who're still alive of course. You've met every single one Mary."

"Then why ask them to Philip's twenty firster?"

"Is that what Jane's doing?"

"It's what she will do" the girl replied. "Oh I've no call to say a word even. But don't you think it rather dim for Philip?"

"I don't know" he said. "Nothing's happened yet surely."

"How d'you mean?"

"I'm still without an invitation and she would be bound to ask me."

"Still you're in bed aren't you? Oh I am so sorry, how horribly rude! I am beastly."

"You aren't" he said. "But of course she'd send an invite even if I couldn't come. We've all stuck together always."

"It's not for me to say but don't you think at his twenty firster Philip ought to see more people of his own age?"

"Of course I don't know who is actually to be invited" he replied. "Do you mean John's going to ask only his cronies to your party?"

"Oh I've got no one, I don't meet a soul" she answered. "You knew Mummy. What would she have done?"

"The same as Jane I imagine."

"She would have invited her."

"Yes" Mr Morris said doubtfully. "Oh yes, at one time."

"You see I was told Daddy and Mrs Weatherby had had a terrific affair once."

Mr Morris seemed uncomfortable.

"Well I don't know about that" he said. "We had our ups and downs. One can't be sure of anything. But what would be wrong if they had?" he asked.

"Oh nothing" she agreed too hastily. "Nothing in the least. Surely I can be curious when I never knew Mummy" she pouted, "don't remember her at all."

"Yes it certainly can't be easy for you" he said.

"I've not known anything else and that's easy" she objected.

Shortly afterwards she left, having learned no more from him.

Later, in time for a glass of sherry, Philip Weatherby sent his name up and was welcomed by Mr Morris.

"Mary's just been" the older man said.

"I'm back from Brighton as a matter of fact and everyone

seems to be asking me if I've come from Mary. I can't understand it."

"You must be thinking of her all the time" Mr Morris replied.

"How's that?"

"Did you never notice Philip? You see someone in the street you haven't met for years and the next fortnight you come across them again and again for a bit. You'd better look out, you're falling in love."

"What's the connection?"

"Forget it I was only joking. There's none of course. Your mother's to give a party I hear."

"Yes she is."

"Your twenty firster?"

"No, just a small thing for her friends. I don't see much point in twenty firsters do you? Or bachelor dinner parties before you're married. All that tripe is out of date."

"Oh I don't know Philip. How about silver weddings?"

"They're different" the young man announced. "They're family. There can be some point in those. But I wanted to ask something. D'you think Mr Pomfret's in love with my mother or her with him?"

"Is she feeding him?"

"What on earth are you getting at?"

"Does she ask him continually to meals. Not drinks, meals."

"Well yes he does come pretty often."

"It's an infallible sign with women Philip. Do you mind?"

"Me? Why should I? It's none of my business. But look here this is strictly private. Was he very much in love with Mamma once?"

"My dear chap I've no way of knowing."

"He was supposed to be wasn't he? Didn't you tell me that?"

"That's not evidence" Mr Morris objected.

"I mean did he ever actually have a child by her?"

Arthur Morris gave the young man a long look before he replied.

"Where is it now if he did?"

"How should I know?"

"Then all you've got is the evidence of your own senses Philip. I wouldn't worry if I were you."

There was no resemblance physical or otherwise between Mr Weatherby and Mary. Shortly after, without another word on this subject, Philip made his excuses and left with ill grace.

LATER THAT WEEK Philip Weatherby and Mary Pomfret were sitting in the downstairs lounge of the same respectable public house off Knightsbridge.

"They all ought to be liquidated" he said obviously in disgust.

"Who Philip?"

"Every one of our parents' generation."

"But I love Daddy."

"You can't."

"I do, so now you know!"

"They're wicked darling" he exclaimed. "They've had two frightful wars they've done nothing about except fight in and they're rotten to the core."

"Barring your relations I suppose?"

"Well Mamma's a woman. She's really not to blame. Nevertheless I do include her. Of course she couldn't manage much about the slaughter. And she can be marvellous at times. Oh I don't know though, I think I hate them every one."

"But why on earth?"

"I feel they're against us."

"You and me do you mean?"

"Well yes if you like. They're so beastly selfish they think of no one and nothing but themselves."

"Are you upset about your twenty firster then?"

"Not really" he answered. "I wouldn't've had one in any case."

"Then what is actually the matter?"

There was a long pause.

"It's because they're like rabbits about sex" he said at last.

"But I don't know the habits of rabbits, do I, except they have delicious noses?"

"You're laughing at me."

"I am a bit."

"But you realise I'm right Mary darling."

"No I don't" she said. "And I'm mad about Daddy."

"Well then what d'you really think about my mother?"

"To me she's very clever and rather sweet, now at all events."

"Even when she practically broke up your mother's home?"

"Oh no Philip you're not to go on this way about parents. If you continue like it you'll begin to have them on your mind and then there'll be rows and all sorts of unpleasantnesses."

"But can you stand by and listen to this talk of theirs without putting in a word?"

"Mummy's dead, we'll never know the truth and it's you who're raking a whole lot up or so I think."

"Oh I didn't have that idea at all" he protested.

"Yet Philip it can only harm Mummy."

"When she was the aggrieved party?" he demanded.

"Of course. You must be discreet you really must."

"I'm sorry. It's natural the whole business should be beastly for you. Forgive me." He sounded genuine and penitent. She smiled rather sadly.

"You're forgiven" she said.

But it appeared he was unable to keep off the subject.

"I went to see Arthur Morris the other day" he began again.

"So did I."

"You did? Yes I think he said something. I've forgotten. But he made the oddest statement. That when a woman starts to get tired of a man she stops feeding him, having him in for real meals."

"If that's so then I truly love Daddy because I what you call feed the dear one all the time."

"We did discuss him as a matter of fact."

"In what way?" she demanded with signs of irritation.

"As to whether Mamma was still fond of your father."

"No Philip you shan't go on like this and you simply mustn't discuss Daddy with Mr Morris. I won't have it d'you hear? You're just raking the ashes and I tell you it's most frightfully suspect."

"I know" he hastened to explain. "I see your point. But I can't sleep at night now, I'm getting in a regular state."

"Oh darling what's the matter?" she asked nervously, and for the first occasion in the evening looked full at him.

"I hope you'll find this absurd, too ridiculous for words, but I've told you before, we might be half brother and sister."

"So you want to make out whether I'm one of your precious relatives?" she asked with scorn.

"Well yes in a way. Yes I do."

"Then I'm not!" she said in almost a loud voice. "I've been making enquiries on my own and we're quite definitely not what you say."

"We aren't?" he cried and it was obvious that he was deeply excited. "You're sure? Certain?"

"Yes Philip."

"But how? Who can possibly tell?"

"Now I'm not going to have another word about that poor wretched worry of yours ever again. And you're to promise me before we leave here!"

"You swear it's true Mary?"

58

"I do" she said. She got out a handkerchief, blew her nose hard. "Now will you promise?"

He showed signs of great nervousness.

"All right. Yes. I will" he said.

She gave him a small smile.

"It's right, what I said. You can trust me" she averred.

"But you went to find out on your own?" he demanded.

"Now you promised you know" she reminded him.

"Yes" he said.

There was a further pause.

"Have another drink?" he asked with enthusiasm at last. "You don't want to go on with those light ales. Try a short."

"I think I'll stick to beer if you do feel like one more" she replied, smiling sadly at him. This time she did not offer to pay the round and sighed as she looked at her face in her mirror while he went to fetch their drinks.

"Have you heard about little Penelope?" he enquired when he came back. He laughed in rather a wild manner.

"No."

"She can't let go of her arm now."

"What do you mean?"

"She will persist in hugging her own elbow Mary. Holds her left arm in the right hand all day, even falls asleep like it at night."

"And how does your mother accept that one?" Miss Pomfret demanded with the first sign of malice she had shown.

"Well I think she's wrong, she takes not the slightest notice Mamma doesn't. But to my mind it might be really serious."

"In what way?" the girl demanded in a bored voice.

"You see I got to the bottom" he replied. "Cheers" he said, raising the glass to his lips. She let her drink stand on the table. "I made Pen come out with it" he went on. "You've no idea the passion for secrecy they have at that age."

59

"I was one once you know" she reminded him.

"By now you must have forgotten" he said. "Well it seems she saw a war-wounded man with a stump for an arm on the front at Brighton without his coat, escaping out of chains or something. So she thinks unless she keeps hold she'll lose hers."

Miss Pomfret yawned.

"I've told Mamma but she won't catch on" he continued. "Mary what do you think?"

"I expect Penelope's doing this to attract attention. Girls usually like attention you know" Miss Pomfret said.

"But if that's the case she'll go on indefinitely."

"I suppose she may Philip."

"That's a grim thought surely?"

"One day she'll marry and then her husband can take over" Miss Pomfret drily suggested.

"Well you know what my mother is. I can't understand her ignoring this. Oh aren't one's parents and their friends extraordinary! Imagine what I overheard between Mamma and that old Abbot. He was going endlessly on about his war experiences out in Italy. She'd said how wonderful she found white oxen. I expect someone once said those great eyes of hers were so like. As a matter of fact I distinctly admire her eyes don't you? But anyway he said he'd spent night after night out with them. That made Mamma scream all right. So he came back that a night in a stall with an ox was a damn sight better than out in the open alone under stars. Then she asked did they snore? Would you believe it? And there's worse coming. Because when he didn't reply Mamma said 'Do they dream Richard?' Honestly I was nearly sick."

"I know" Miss Pomfret agreed. "They can be frightful."

Mrs Weatherby was giving Mary's father dinner.

"Oh my dear" she said "when are we ever going to see the sun?" He sighed.

"Is there simply never to be Spring this year?" she insisted.

"The continual rain is too frightful" Mr Pomfret agreed. "Well Jane was your trip down to Brighton a success?"

"It helped Penelope and me so enormously John."

"Did you see anyone?" he incuriously enquired.

"Richard Abbot came over for the day which was sweet of him wasn't it? Oh yes Philip was kind enough to look in."

"And how's Pen?"

"Ah the gallant angel" Jane cried. "She's my one comfort apart from you. She loved Brighton. Just came back with a little thing, only that she has somehow to keep hold on her elbow, but I know a way to manage the little sweet. I'm going to buy her a bag, John, to carry. Now don't you think that a brilliant notion?"

"Well well" he said, not to commit himself. "And Philip?"

"Oh no, there I'm in despair" she announced. "Simply desperate."

"Would you like me to talk to him?"

"Dear John I've changed my mind" she said. "I think I'd really rather not, that you didn't. It was poor Richard offered himself you remember and put it in my head. Of course I thought at once how much better you would be if you could. But the boy's been so disagreeable, John. Don't remind me of him please."

"He hasn't been rude to you?"

"Oh no not quite. It's just I think he's insane. Better leave him strictly to his poor mad self. And you? How have you been?"

"As well as may be these hard times."

"How true that is darling. But then Mary? What's her news?"

"I don't seem to see much of her Jane. One's offspring are a sacred farce."

"John you don't think this extraordinary feeling they have for snobbery, some of them that is because I'm sure I've not noticed the tiniest trace, even, in Mary, can you suppose it would go oh I can't tell but to absurd lengths with them, even to refusing to marry outside the family."

"What've you got in mind? The old continental requirement of sixteen quarterings in a husband?"

"No no my dear I wish I had" she said. "Or rather I think it quite out of date don't you and in any case I haven't any, that is I can't run to that extraordinary number. But of course in a small way it might simplify things."

"How Jane?"

"Well naturally not with my Philip" she explained in a laugh. "He's got the idea now right enough. Yet I've warned him it might cut both ways, prevent his marrying someone he very much wanted. And again I don't mean Mary, I'm sure the dear child is much too sensible. But oh John I have warned Philip if not once then quite a thousand times. No but the whole picture has grown so enormous in his poor head I really believe he feels deep down inside him that he must, simply must find a wife so close that the marriage could almost turn out to be incestuous John."

"Incestuous. So you're afraid he'll never start a family is that it?" Mr Pomfret did not appear to take the conversation seriously.

At this point Mrs Weatherby left her place to twitter in bad Italian down the dumbwaiter shaft. She was answered by a sweet babble that was almost song.

"Ah these Southerners" the lady remarked as she sat herself at table again. "The other day Isabella came to me for half a crown. The last occasion she asked for money was only the whole return fare to go back to Italy to vote in the elections. So I naturally wanted to know what for this time

and what d'you suppose she said, why simply to buy a
mouse. 'Get a mouse?' I said after I'd looked the word
up in the dictionary. 'Because Roberto' that's our cat 'is
so lonely' she answered. I screamed, I just yelled, wouldn't
you? I can't bear cruelty to animals John dear. But she's
so persistent and in the end of course she got her own
way! Naturally I kept out of the house for a few days
after that and forbad sweet Penelope the kitchen or I said
I'd simply never speak to the child again. And then I
forgot. Isn't it dreadful the way one does? I went down
there for something or other and Isabella showed me.
They were both drinking milk out of the same saucer,
Roberto and his mouse. John is it sorcery, spell-binding
or something?"

He laughed. "No I'd heard of that before dear Jane."

"You truly had? Sometimes, lying in my lonely lonely
bed at night I wonder if I just imagine I'm alive and all these
queer things are true. Because I don't like to say it but Philip
is simply very odd. He asks me the most extraordinary
questions John."

"Does he now?"

"Oh I don't want to go into things" she said in haste.
"Were we like that once dear?" she asked. Then "are we
never to be served?" she demanded with hardly a pause and
in the same voice. At which she called from the table an
unintelligible phrase in which she displayed great confidence
to be answered by an understanding, distant shout.

"Mary's been displaying quite an interest lately" he suggested.

"Has she? Now you know you have really something there
in that girl" she said. "Mary's such a sweet child."

"Thank you Jane" he replied. "Yes" he went on "she
seems quite taken up with the past for the present, no pun
intended."

"What past?"

"Ours of course" he answered. "What other could she
wish to learn at eighteen? She wants to know the who's

who of all our friends and to find out even if you and I didn't see a deal of each other at one time."

"Well I don't know if I'd care . . ." Mrs Weatherby murmured.

"And you don't imagine I'd blurt I don't know what out to me own daughter?" Mr Pomfret demanded. "No what's over is over."

"Maybe for you perhaps" she responded. "Oh how must it be to be a man?"

"Trousers my dear are very uncomfortable. I wish I wore skirts. No honestly since my tailor lost his cutter to a bomb in the war I haven't been able to sit down to meals in comfort, it's frightful."

"Would you like to go out for a minute then since we never seem to be going to get anything to eat?"

"What and leave you on your own darling?" he cried. "At the mercy of a foreign language you hardly understand?"

"I speak Italian quite nicely now thank you" she smiled. "And do you know, I've never had a single lesson."

"Don't don't" he wailed. "When I think of the daily woman who changes every two months and who what she calls cooks for us."

"My poor John you should have someone to look after you" Mrs Weatherby said obviously delighted.

"Oh Mary's very good" he said at once. "It's not her fault you know."

"I do realise, who could understand better than me?" she exclaimed. "If I hadn't always been so quick with languages I'd be in the same boat" she cried. "But it's not the children's fault, John. We could travel, try our accents out and they still can't."

"Mary's very good" he said "only she won't get me jugged hare."

"Jugged hare?" Mrs Weatherby echoed in plain desperation. "Jugged hare! Oh my dear does that mean you are very difficult about it? Because that's precisely what I'm giving you this evening."

Her lovely eyes filled with tears. He got to his feet, went round to the back of her and kissed a firm cheek while she held her face up to him.

"My perfect woman" he said.

"But should I have remembered?"

"You have" he answered sitting down again. "My favourite dish."

"That's just it John oh dear" she cried. "You're an expert, you've tried jugged hare in all your clubs and now here's poor me offering it to you cooked by a Neapolitan who probably thinks the jugged part comes out of a jar in spite of all I poured out to her about port wine! And I tried to teach her so hard darling. There's still time to change though. Would you like some eggs instead?"

"But I told you" he replied eyes gleaming "you've picked my favourite. Jane this is a red letter evening."

"I only hope it will be" she said at her most dry. "We're still at the stage of just having had the soup. Some more wine John?" and she passed the bottle then went to shout down the shaft.

"*Io furiosa*" she yelled "*Isabella!*"

A long wail in Italian was the answer.

"No don't darling, I can smell it at last" Mr Pomfret laughed. "And it is going to be delicious."

At the same great hotel in which they held their Sunday luncheons Mrs Weatherby reserved a private room to entertain old friends in honour of Philip's twenty firster.

Standing prepared, empty, curtained, shuttered, tall mirrors facing across laid tables crowned by napkins, with space rocketing transparence from one glass silvered surface to the other, supporting walls covered in olive coloured silk, chandeliers repeated to a thousand thousand profiles to be lost in olive gray depths as quiet as this room's untenanted attention, but a scene made warm with mass upon mass of daffodils banked up against mirrors, or mounded once on each of the round white tables and laid in a flat frieze about their edges, – here then time stood still for Jane, even in wine bottles over to one side holding the single movement, and that unseen of bubbles rising just as the air, similarly trapped even if conditioned, watched unseen across itself in a superb but not indifferent pause of mirrors.

Into this waiting shivered one small seen movement that seemed to snap the room apart, a door handle turning.

Then with a cry unheard, sung now, unuttered then by hinges and which fled back to creation in those limitless centuries of staring glass, with a shriek only of silent motion the portals came ajar with as it were an unoperated clash of cymbal to usher Mrs Weatherby in, her fine head made tiny by the intrusion perhaps because she was alone, but upon which, as upon a rising swell of violas untouched by bows strung from none other than the manes of unicorns that quiet wait was ended, the room could gather itself up at last.

As after a pause of amazement she stepped through, murmuring over a shoulder *"oh my darlings"* the picture she made there, and it was a painting, was echoed a thousand thousand times; strapless shoulders out of a full gray dress that was flounced and soft but from which her shoulders rose still softer up to eyes over which, and the high forehead, dark wings of her hair were folded rather as a raven may claim for itself the evening air, the chimes, the quiet flight back home to rest.

"How good of Gaspard" Jane said with an awed voice. At which Philip and Mary entered in their turn. The boy switched on more light.

"No don't" Mrs Weatherby reproved in the same low tones. "You'll spoil it all" she said.

"But it's lovely" Miss Pomfret murmured.

Pascal sidled through the door which he closed, then turned the lights down again until the room held its original illumination, and there was now the difference made by this intrusion of bare arms and women's shoulders. Mary studied hers in a mirror she had reached. Dressed in black with no jewelry the similar milk white of her face and chest was thinner, watered down beside Mrs Weatherby's full cream of flesh which seemed to retain a satisfied glow of the well fed against Mary's youth starvation. But there was this about the whites of Miss Mary Pomfret's eyes, they were a blue beyond any previously blessed upon humanity by Providence compared with the other ladies present, and it was perhaps to these sweet rounds of early nights that her own attention turned because Jane's were red veined as leaves.

"Is Madame satisfied?" Pascal asked, almost one old friend to another, his false restaurant accent forgotten at this minute.

"Monsieur Medrano you are truly wonderful" the lady said. "When I had to sell my precious brooch to give the evening I didn't know – how could I tell . . ." she faltered, and he could see her eyes fill with tears.

"We have done my best for Madame" the great man answered. "Madame is more beautiful than ever" he proudly announced. "I say to Gaspard, 'Gaspard' I said 'let all be as never before my friend because you know who will be taking our Parma rooms tonight.'"

"No don't – you mustn't – I shall really cry in a moment" Mrs Weatherby exclaimed from the heart. "But it is perfect!"

"Jolly good" her son brought out.

"Ah Philip please not, I'm sorry to be so rude, you see you'll ruin this perfect thing! There do just be content to be an angel and simply place the cards."

Pascal made small adjustments to napkins folded into linen crowns.

"You did tell the chef about our *soufflé?*" Mrs Weatherby asked eventually.

When the great man replied he used the restaurateur's manner.

"He said it over to me by heart, by heart I made him repeat, Madame. And we have a small favour to ask Madame. We will order orchids for the ladies, gardenias for the gentlemen if you please?"

"But Pascal good Heavens my bill!"

"The management they come to me" he proclaimed "they say 'it is not often we have with us Mrs Weatherby Medrano.' They remember Madame. No no Madame if you will allow us it is on the 'otel" he said.

"It's too much, children have you heard? Pascal you must thank Mr Poinsetta very specially from me. No I will come tomorrow myself!" She fingered daffodils here and there on the top table, not to disarrange these but almost as though to reassure herself that all were true, to prove to her own satisfaction that she was not bewitched.

"I shall be at call" Pascal said and sidled out. Mrs Weatherby followed him with her eyes. When the door was quite shut she turned the glance on Mary who was still examining herself in a glass. The older woman stared.

"My dear you look sweet" she gravely said.

"Doesn't she" Philip answered from his task.

"Do I?" the girl said and turned to him.

Mrs Weatherby frowned.

"Wonderful" she echoed. "And isn't it good of you to come so soon to help. I always feel nervous, distracted before a party I'm giving. And now this divine place has truly done us proud! Philip I wonder if you realise there aren't many women in London they'd put themselves out for in this heavenly way."

Her son looked up, the seating list in one hand. "You're telling me" he said. "Look Mamma you've a card here" he waved it "and there's no mention of him on my plan. Mr William Smith."

"Nonsense my dear, poor William's dead these ages past."

"Well there's his card."

"Give it here Philip. That must be an old one. Why it's all yellow. How odd and sad" she tore the thing up into very small bits. She looked about for an ashtray. "How dreadful" she murmured. "Philip you didn't do this to me?"

"Never heard of the man" he replied with what was obviously truth.

"Mary my dear I wonder if I might bother you" Mrs Weatherby suggested brightly. "Such a shame to leave these pieces when everything's fresh! Of course there is behind my daffodils in the fireplace but I rather think not don't you, I never like to look the other side of anything in hotels. Could you be sweet and put them right outside?"

Mary received those pieces, was reaching for the handle, when the door opened and her father's head appeared.

"Well here we are" he cried at his most jovial. "Hello my love" he said to his daughter as she passed him. "Jane my dear, me dear" he boomed then strode towards her.

She offered him a cheek. While he kissed she pushed hers

just the once sharply back at him. She did the same when he kissed the other side.

"Dear darling John how kind" she cried. "D'you think I did right? I said I wouldn't have Eduardo to announce the guests. After all we do all know each other don't we?"

"As long as they find the way dear. I notice Mary has. Until I found her note at home I distinctly thought we were to come on to this together."

"It's been such true kindness in her to arrive early and help" Mrs Weatherby insisted. "No the cloakroom people will tell stragglers where we are. And then I shall send Philip out to round them up. But haven't they done me proud darling?"

"Why but you're the only person out of all London tonight Jane! Even at this sad hotel they realise that."

"You're such a comfort indeed! Philip have you finished with those cards?" At which Mary Pomfret ushered Richard Abbot through the door. "Oh Dick!" their hostess cried.

"I say I say" he said as he advanced and kissed both her cheeks in turn while she pushed sharply twice back, at him. "Well look at you" he exclaimed gazing fondly on her. "Wonderful eh?" he demanded and ended with a "Simply astounding!"

"But which?" she demanded radiant. "The room or me?"

"God bless my soul, both. No, here, what am I saying? Dear Jane" he said "could there be a choice? I mean with you standing there! Hello John. Seems we're a bit early aren't we you and I?"

"Darling Richard" she murmured. "Oh I'm so lucky!"

Then another male guest entered. Mrs Weatherby greeted him with warmth but gave the man no more than the one cheek which she held immovable and firm under great mischievous eyes.

The party had begun.

HALF THE GUESTS had put in an appearance before Miss Jennings presented herself looking sadly pretty and also, on closer inspection, quite considerably upset.

As Liz made her way to greet the hostess through a small crowd of company drinking cocktails John Pomfret came forward, as if breasting the calls with which Miss Jennings greeted so many friends in order to give her special welcome. She did not pause but hissed,

"Oh my dear where have you been? I phoned you all day," and then found herself before Mrs Weatherby, to burst into exclamations, to praise, to receive praises until she had her chance alone for a moment with Jane.

"Darling d'you know what that beastly Maud Winder's said? That I was tipsy at Eddie's dance."

"But I've never heard anything so frightful in my life" this lady cried albeit in a careful, restrained voice. "Oh my dear how criminal of Maud!"

"Isn't it? I think I could hate that woman Jane. Have you invited her tonight?"

"If I'd only been told" Mrs Weatherby exclaimed with caution. "What can I say? But Eddie's here and he won't move without her" as another I could mention without someone else, her wary eye expressed unheard to be taken up silently again and again in tall mirrors.

"Then you could ask him if she told the truth. No Jane I do so wish you would" Miss Jennings implored with open signs of agitation.

"As though I should even dream of such a thing! Liz your worst enemy, not that you have one in the whole wide world darling would never conceive of anything horrible like that." Upon which, well out of sight down along a plump firm thigh Mrs Weatherby crossed two fingers.

"But isn't it terrible . . . ?" Liz began and had to stand back for a newly arrived couple who came up to go through the shrill ritual of delighted cries at Jane's appearance, at their own reaction to the flattery she repaid with interest, and at the blossoming, the to them so they said incredible conjuring up out of these perfect flowers, of a Spring lost once more for yet another year to the sad denizens of London in rain fog mist and cold. When these two had drifted off Miss Jennings was able to start afresh.

"As if I ever did drink, really drink I mean. Oh my dear and I was so looking forward to this heavenly evening!"

"You must put it quite out of your sweet head" Mrs Weatherby proclaimed with emphasis while she smiled and nodded when she caught a guest's already perhaps rather over-bright eye. "I shall speak to.Maud myself. This is too bad."

"I'm not at her table oh do say not!"

"I wouldn't dream of such a thing you're with us John and me of course" upon which Miss Jennings with a hint of timidity in her bearing as if she'd just heard yet another insinuation against her security had once more to step back while a second couple paid respect. Then when these two had done with Jane they descended for an endless minute on Miss Jennings until at last they picked their way off towards the drinks.

"My dear can't I get Philip to fetch you just a little one?" Mrs Weatherby asked.

"And leave Maud Winder draw her own conclusions?" the younger woman wailed. "Because if you had sat us down a place away from each other then I really believe I'd have had to beg you to change round the cards."

Jane put on a stern look.

"Liz darling you can take these things too far" she begged. "Oh what haven't I suffered myself in my time from idle tongues! Why only the other day my own child came to me with some extraordinary tale that I'm sure I'd never heard ever but about me of course. Sometimes I think stories of that kind hang about like nasty smells in old cupboards and I'm sure are just as hard to get rid of. Forget all about it, I know I have. The mere suggestion with someone

73

like you darling is too ridiculous for words. And I always say when I see a man drink cider at meals that means he can't trust himself."

"Maybe I will have a weak one then."

"Philip" Mrs Weatherby waved. "Philip! Martini or sherry?"

"Oh perhaps a sherry please."

"My dear boy Miss Jennings has nothing to drink! You must keep moving around you know. Liz would like a sherry and I think I'll try one of those martinis. Oh dear I'll be drunk as a fish wife if I do, but hang it's what I say, might as well be hung for a lamb or whatever the silly phrase is Liz don't you agree, you must!"

"But for one to be said one is when you aren't!"

"Now you promised Liz darling!"

"When I haven't ever in my life" the young woman persisted.

"Darling" Mrs Weatherby warned with a hint of impatience.

"Oh I know I'm a bore" Miss Jennings cried. "How dreadful and you must please forgive! You see . . ." but yet another pair of new arrivals were making their way and as Jane advanced to meet these she gave Liz one of those long looks of love and expiation for which she was justly famous.

Miss Jennings went after John Pomfret.

"Where have you been all day?" she demanded when she had cornered him apart.

"This endless work work work" he answered.

"Not in your own office, that I do know" she cried.

"Precisely" he said. "Time was one could sit in one's room, do all which had to be done in comparative comfort. But no longer, not now any more!"

"And I did want you so! Must it always be like this?"

"How d'you mean? Liz is something the matter?"

"Just that beastly Maud Winder. She only said I was tight at Eddie's!"

"If she did then she's half seas over now herself!"

"Can the awful woman be here? I don't see her. No John don't be so absurd."

"But there" he said of a Mrs Winder who seemed dead sober in quiet conversation with her back to a mirror. "Tight as a coot."

"Well talk of the devil" Miss Jennings exclaimed. "Really I feel that if it weren't for Jane I ought to go up and slap that silly face. Do you honestly think she's drunk?"

"If she isn't quite now, she has been" he replied. "Something must have gone very wrong with her end of Eddie's party which brought her to repeat what she did, if in fact she did."

"Oh Arthur Morris told me."

"What a shame old Arthur can't be here."

"Yes" she said. "And a terrible story to insinuate against a girl!"

"Look Liz" he implored "forget the whole of this."

"You're asking me dear?" she demanded.

"Because I was with you Liz and you were sober as a judge."

"But that only makes everything all the worse."

"Naturally it does" he cheerfully agreed. "And so now then?"

"Do you truly love me?" she enquired.

"Of course I do."

"Are you sure?"

"Liz darling!"

"Well perhaps I'll just find myself able to last out" she said. "As long as the wretched woman doesn't dare speak to me that is. I could claw her heart right away from her flat chest."

"Well Liz a wonderful show of Jane's by God eh?" a voice announced behind and she turned to find Richard Abbot. "Marvellous manager" he went on. "Can't imagine how she gets such details organised these days. Upon my soul it's perfectly miraculous!"

"I know Richard" Miss Jennings replied with an animated look. "And to see all one's nearest and dearest gathered in one room why it's unique! I do admire Jane so, she's a positive genius."

"Tell you what" Mr Abbot propounded. "A thousand pities poor old Arthur can't be present."

"I've a wire from him in my pocket this moment wishing us all the best of good times" John Pomfret said. "They handed it me outside."

"Has he telegraphed to Jane I wonder?" Liz thought aloud. "She would like it because this is her party after all."

"Oh the wire's for her all right. She doesn't know yet."

"Then let me take the thing along old boy" Mr Abbot asked in a proprietary voice. "Might buck her up a bit. Sure to be feeling a trifle nervous before the curtain rises so to speak."

"Why certainly" John responded reaching into his "tails". "I could have done that myself" he said with a trace of irony. He handed the envelope over.

"But I say" Richard Abbot expostulated. "It's been opened."

"I told you what was inside didn't I old man?"

"I mean how am I to explain to her?"

"Just tell her it was me Richard."

"You opened a telegram addressed to Jane?" Miss Jennings demanded.

"I thought there might be a bit of bad news which could keep until the party was over" he told her in an almost insolent manner.

"Well you can keep the damn thing, break your own good tidings" Mr Abbot exploded without raising his voice and handed the envelope back. "Yes by God" he said then left them.

"He seemed quite upset" Mr Pomfret remarked.

"I'm not sure I quite like you in this mood" she warned.

"Oh come off your high horse Liz" he laughed. "You know I simply can't stand the fellow, pompous ass that the man is."

WHEN DINNER WAS well under way, with servants hurrying about the round tables, John Pomfret Liz Richard Abbot and our hostess alone at theirs, the laughing and conversation everywhere at a great pitch, so Jane delighting with all her soul broke out with the following comment on what they themselves had chanced in their own chatter,

"Oh, isn't all this delicious my dears and doesn't it seem only the other day that we were deep in the topic of sex instruction for each other's children and here we are now in an argument about whether they ought to live out in rooms for freedom."

"Bachelors shouldn't speak up I expect, but part of the idea was the young people might get used to living on what they earn surely?" Mr Abbot genially enquired.

"Darling Richard so unromantic" Mrs Weatherby crowed. "Don't you remember John years ago you got in such a state and I was to make a gramophone record for your Mary, oh wouldn't she have hated it, while in return you were to do one for Philip. Then we thought we'd advertise and have a truly immense sale to the public."

"And I took you to the place in Oxford Street when soon as we got inside a glass box we were tongue tied" John added.

They all laughed.

"Then what did you do?" Liz demanded.

"Why nothing of course" Mr Pomfret cried. "That is the whole beauty of us, we never can seem to do anything."

Jane dabbed at her eyes.

"What could a woman say to a schoolboy without making him feel such a perfect fool?" she demanded ecstatically. "But I worried like mad then didn't I John?"

"Bet you couldn't have" Mr Abbot said adoring.

"Oh yes I did" Jane assured him. "Tell me darlings isn't this being such a huge success? Don't you think it was a rather marvellous idea of mine to have them all at tables for four? As long as we insist on a general post with the coffee. You two men must start that ball rolling. Why I can hardly hear myself speak they make so terrific a racket!"

"The greatest fun Jane" Mr Pomfret assured her. Indeed it would have been difficult for any such party to go better.

"Well I was never told a thing" Liz said.

"Why you're to stay here of course. I don't intend us to move."

"I meant about sex Jane."

"No more was I" this lady wailed.

"And I've a flat of my own which I can promise hasn't made all that difference."

"My dear you are between the two generations you fortunate angel! It's these children I'm so worried over. Now John you started the argument. What d'you say to Liz?"

"If our children were all like her we'd not need to discuss anything" he laughed. "What's your opinion Richard?" he asked a bit hastily.

"Younger generation's all right I suppose" Mr Abbot temporised.

"But the sweet ones simply aren't" Mrs Weatherby beamed at him. "You know my dear you've been a weeny shade selfish all your life not having children. Though I do love you for it."

"Know nothing about 'em" he said.

"Yet you should, a great goodlooking man like you! It's unfair."

"When I said that, Jane, I didn't infer every parent I'm acquainted with doesn't come to me for advice" he riposted.

"Good for you Richard" Mr Pomfret cried. "You had us there."

The champagne they were drinking was plentiful.

"And me too" Liz claimed, as if she would not be left out.

"In that case I expect my dears you two know far more than any of us, mothers and fathers that we are" Mrs Weatherby laughed. "We're so ashamed we don't dare ask except, though I say who shouldn't, at some heavenly party like this."

"Oh no Jane" Mr Pomfret objected. "You go too far. Mary's always been sweet. I'm ashamed of myself where she's concerned."

"But you know very well what I didn't mean darling" Mrs Weatherby cried. "Good heavens I simply never mean anything yet all my life I've got into such frightful trouble with my tongue."

"Certainly going like a house on fire" Mr Abbot said as he looked around the room.

"Oh aren't I fortunate to have such divine friends" Jane cried. "Still, all joking apart my Philip really should take the plunge and launch off into a flat of his own."

"Can he afford it?" Miss Jennings wanted to be told.

"Gracious me I only meant a little room somewhere. The poor sweet mustn't be expected to fly before he's able to walk should he? Darling Maud Winder who can be so naughty sometimes, her girl is on her own. They all do it now and it might have been everything for us if we had been allowed couldn't that be so John?"

Mrs Weatherby found Richard Abbot gazing at her with a pleading expression.

"What I'm trying to say" she went on "simply is if Philip won't ask girls to the house then he should go somewhere they can just force themselves upon him."

"And if one fine day you found a mother ringing your door bell whose daughter he'd got in the family way?" Mr Abbot asked.

"Oh my dear don't! But how barbarous of you Richard! Wouldn't that be just the end! Yet I hardly think Philip could. Oh what have I said? I don't mean what's just slipped out at all. I'm sure he's perfectly normal. It's his principles you see. He's too high principled to live!" Mrs Weatherby turned a shy look on John Pomfret. "What d'you feel dear?" she suggested.

"Well things are different with girls I suppose" he said. "I think females ought to share with another woman friend."

"So does Maud's Elaine."

"I know Jane" Liz interrupted "but how does that alter matters? She's no more than exchanging her mother for a girl her own age."

"The friend needn't always be in" Mrs Weatherby said with a look of unease and distress.

"Nor need a father or mother dear."

"Yes Liz how perfectly right you are as always. But I'm convinced they could arrange for one or the other to be out sometimes! Think of the horrid awkwardness of fixing that up with a parent!!"

"It's worse when the parent has to implore his child not to be home at certain hours" John Pomfret said, a remark which was received in silence.

"Awkward lives you family people do seem to lead" Mr Abbot propounded. They all roared their laughter.

"How perfectly wicked of you Dick" Mrs Weatherby approved.

Pomfret said "My trouble is I never seem to hear of any girl who wants to share a room or two, do you?"

"Ought I d'you think?" Liz demanded.

"My dear" Mr Pomfret hastened to assure her "I didn't – I mean I wasn't fishing to get Mary in your flat."

"That just didn't enter my head. What I meant John was, should I still continue to live alone? D'you believe that does make people talk even nowadays?"

"How about me?" Abbot enquired heavily. "Can my reputation stand it?"

80

"Now Richard" Mrs Weatherby remonstrated with some firmness. "Humour is not your long suit you know. I don't think what you're pretending a bit funny my dear."

"I can't see why everything should be different for men" Miss Jennings objected.

"Because they're expected to have women in and I imagine in all my innocence we're not supposed to have men" Jane said.

"I know that of course" Liz replied emptying her glass. "But I still don't see the big blot. If there's no more to it than low gossip then, while dreadful enough of course, should one change one's whole life round just for that?"

"I'd have thought there was a question of children" Mr Abbot explained. "Women having babies eh?"

"Richard" Mrs Weatherby cried in great good humour but in a stern voice. "Do please don't become coarse! Men can have children too can't they?"

"Dreadfully sorry and all that but girls do saddle themselves with the little things, have done since the start of time."

"Not Mary though" Jane said.

"No Richard's perfectly right" John assured them. "The danger must be greater as you yourself admitted when you confessed you'd not care to have an outraged mother at your bell, the heavy expectant daughter at her heels. After all Liz you can look after yourself."

"Can I?" she interjected and was ignored.

"Now what we were discussing" Mr Pomfret went on "was how to gently ease the fledglings from the downy nest. They have to learn to fly some time. I know Mary will be all right but Jane doesn't want Philip a runner."

"Darling my boy's not won a race in his life."

"Wounded bird, broken wing Jane" Mr Abbot explained.

THE YOUNG PEOPLE for Philip's twenty firster consisted of Philip Weatherby Mary Pomfret Elaine Winder and the youth she had brought with her, Derek Wolfram. These four made up one of the round tables.

Elaine had drawn attention to Miss Jennings to ask if her name was what it was. On being assured this could be so, she enquired whether Liz was a particular friend of anyone present; Philip looked at Mary, had no sign, kept silent, and Miss Winder then continued,

"Well my children" she said "the way some women do go on! I saw this with my own sore eyes. Mummy had taken me to a certain party. We brought along a bottle of champagne as a matter of fact which turned out to be a bit of a swindle because no one else had, in fact a woman old enough to be my grandmother just took one of vermouth. There's nothing cheaper surely, I mean you have to pay more for orangeade don't you? Anyway there was this person, Miss Jennings, right next me on a sofa where I'd managed to tuck myself in because there was not a soul for me about, it was one of these so called literary do's, God no! I was listening to a conversation she was having with a type who'd sat himself down between, no friend of mine good Lord, I wouldn't have touched him with a barge pole but anyway there he was and he seemed to know her and that was that when suddenly I heard him say, 'can't I get you another drink' and she mumbled something although I didn't take particular notice at the time if you know what I mean. But to cut a long story short" Miss Winder ended tamely, perhaps rather daunted by the degree the others were paying attention which possibly she was not always accustomed to receive, Miss Elaine Winder said "well anyway the lady was sozzled and Mummy who was in the doorway, saw her trip over the rug later and be carried off. Properly – no I don't know it may have been rucked up and she'd caught her toe, I can't tell, wish you'd been there

Derek, Lord I had a lousy time. I say are we going to dance after?"

THESE ROUND TABLES were large enough to allow one couple to talk without the other hearing what passed.

Maybe it was on account of the champagne or possibly because Jane and John seemed to be rather wrapped up in one another but Dick Abbot said to Liz,

"I say you know but you look perfectly ravishing tonight."

"I do?"

"You certainly are."

"Well thanks very much Richard" she responded.

"Makes me feel so embarrassed talking about the younger generation in front of you" he continued. "Lord you're a part of 'em yet we go on as if you weren't there. Can't think what you must make of us."

"You're such a friendly person" Miss Jennings announced. "Richard I feel so at home with you!"

"You do? I'm honoured Liz. Nicest thing one can be told, that. But of course I haven't the airs and graces."

"I don't know what you mean by it! When I find a person's cosy that's all I ask. Because what are we here for? Life's not so wonderful surely that we can afford to miss any single chance – not to help the lame dog over a stile, I don't mean, it seems so disobliging to draw attention in that way somehow, I mean about being lame, as practically no one is except poor Arthur Morris; now where was I – oh yes what I'm trying to explain is we've each one of us simply got to stay careful for each other don't you feel or we're absolutely nothing, I mean lower than the lowest worm that crawls?"

83

"Always say must respect the next man or Richard you've had it."

"But I can't get the extraordinary phrase you used about your not having the social graces whatever that may add up to although I believe I understand quite well because of course real politeness which is only fellow feeling, isn't it, is no more than that; all I'm trying to say, you see, is if a person's cosy it's perfection, true manners, what distinguishes us from animals."

"Jolly though when a cat curls up on one's knee."

"Yes and then they go spitting in each other's faces soon as the moon is up and they've found a brick wall. Oh one can't trust them Richard, that is what's so awful but you've only to look into their eyes don't you agree, just like goats?"

"Don't know, you know. I'm very partial to a cat."

"Well take birds then. What could be sweeter than a robin redbreast yet there's someone been studying them, did you read the book, and they're the fiercest things alive he says, would you believe it?"

"Jungle law" the man agreed.

"And some of these debs" she went on. "Since you were speaking of their generation weren't you? Why I could tell stories but I'm simply not that sort of person. With sleek heads and skins and no knowledge of the world, of how people can count to one another I mean, – well some of them are no better than goats there you are, than farm yard goats."

"Remember I passed two common women once outside a pub and one said to the other 'you filthy Irish git.'"

"What's a git then?" she enquired.

"Goat" he replied.

"How truly curious" she agreed. "But you do see this my way?" she proceeded. "Oh Richard it is so rare to find a man who looks through the surface as you can, deep down to what really's there." She lowered her voice, glanced over to Jane and John still engrossed in themselves then hitched her chair closer to Mr Abbot's. "Life" she continued "is not all going back on one's tracks, ferreting out old friends to have a cosy chat with, one simply can't for ever be looking over a shoulder Richard to what's dead and gone. Such a blind view of life. No, you have to look forward, face the future whatever that may bring."

"No friend like an old friend" he claimed.

"You're not on to what I mean" she said. "Take John now. There are times I could shake him, just shake him. You know what they were once supposed to mean to one another and never will again those two, well as if that wasn't enough he's always going back. He won't admit if you ask him but he's got an idea that once he's had anything in his life he's only to lift his voice to get that back once more and dear Jane's too sweet to let him see."

"Wonderful woman Jane."

"Isn't she?" Miss Jennings sighed. She drank down a full glass of wine. "Too sweet and wonderful. Sometimes. Any other woman would say 'Now look John dear I admit we once meant everything to each other and you practically broke your wife's heart over me, but all of it's been finished a long time now, happened many lovers' moons ago and can't come to life again, these little things never do'."

"I say Liz you know, none of my business" Mr Abbot warned.

"But what does she say?" his companion continued. "Jane's forever calling Penelope 'her little saint' but Jane is the saint if you get me or isn't she?"

"Oh a saint yes undoubtedly."

"How can Jane put up with him in one of those moods! Now I, I think it's bad for John all this rehashing of what's dead and gone, I try to take his mind off which is the reason I'm such a good influence. I truly am the man's guardian angel."

"Tremendously lucky fellow."

"Not but what it can't be a great strain at times" she

murmured with a tragic expression. "No one in the whole wide world can have the least idea. I get the feeling occasionally, oh to tell the utter truth because I know you are like the grave it is more than that, I wouldn't say quite often but continually I have to lug poor John back to the present by main force and I'm not very strong. It wears me out."

"Shouldn't let yourself get upset like this, a splendid little woman like you young enough to be his daughter."

"I suppose it's like so many men" she gave judgement aloud "who imagine no girl can look at a male older than herself. But you're wrong, think of history, anything! As a matter of fact to tell you a little secret about me which I truly trust you not to breathe, I've always been attracted to older men."

"Have you by Jove!"

"Yes, isn't that strange. But I don't like little old men, they have to be great big hussars if they are older. So now you know!"

"Not for me" he said. "I go for the young ones."

"Oh no you can't mean little girls" she cried. "Pig-tails and tunics!"

"I say what must you think Liz" he expostulated. "Nothing of the sort. I should hope not. No to tell the truth it's young women of your age, young but old enough to be women if you get what I mean."

"Jane" she enthusiastically cried "Richard's just paid me the sweetest compliment! He's said what he likes about me is I'm young but with all the allure of experience!!"

"My dear how clever of Richard" Mrs Weatherby drily rejoined.

"No not all that" Miss Jennings appealed to the wine waiter who was filling her glass to the brim once more only she didn't lift it to stop him. Mr Pomfret slightly raised his eyebrows, then Jane and he descended back into their own conversation to the exclusion of all else.

"But I think it's one of the nicest things have ever been

said to me" she purred at Mr Abbot. "I feel just like one of your cats when you've given her cream."

"True right enough" he stoutly averred.

"It had the ring of truth" Miss Jennings said. "Everything you say has, I think that's my real reason why I like you so. You're such a wonderfully honest person Richard."

"Can't understand people saying what they don't mean. Doesn't make sense."

"And honest about yourself" she continued "which is the rarest thing in the world, pure gold."

IT WAS ALMOST AS IF, in time, the party had leaped forward between those mirrors so much had been recorded only to be lost, so much champagne had been consumed while, as day passes over a pond, no trace was left in any of their minds, or hardly none, just the vague memory of friendly weather, a fading riot of June stayed perhaps in their throats as the waiters withdrew though three or four remained to serve coffee brandy and port.

This was the moment chosen by Philip Weatherby to make his empty tumbler ring to a stroke of the knife, to rise with one hand of Mary's in his own while she stayed seated, to look so white as he examined the guests from the advantage he had taken, that of surprise and the five foot ten of height.

"Oh the dear boy" his mother said to John Pomfret. "He's going to propose my health, or so I do believe the saint."

"I – ah – er" her son began while Miss Pomfret squeezed Philip's fingers.

"But who put it in his sweet head?" Mrs Weatherby asked

entranced. "Darling was this your idea?" she demanded and had no answer.

"I – well you see – that is . . ." Mr Weatherby began again while all the older people looked up at him with smiling faces, with that kind of withdrawn encouragement we use by which to judge how much better we could do this sort of thing ourselves, and Jane beamed as if in a seventh heaven. "Ladies and gentlemen" he tried once more "we are here tonight to celebrate my twenty firster." He now started to speak very fast. "My mother which is kind of her gave this party" he went on "and I'm sure we've all very much enjoyed things, the festive occasion and so on, but Mary and I thought now or never which is why we want to announce that we're engaged."

He sat down. A hum of fascinated comment was directed like bees to honey in his direction. Mary hardly glanced at her father but darted quick looks about the room while Jane turned to John Pomfret, one hand pressed to the soft mound above her heart and hissed,

"Is this your doing? Did you know of it?"

"Good God good for them. First I've heard" he said.

"Oh my dear" she cried. "I feel faint!"

Not that Mr Pomfret appeared to pay heed. A pale smile was stuck across his face while he looked about as though to receive tribute. But the attention of almost everyone in that room was still fixed on the awkward happy couple, and Elaine Winder smacked their backs and generally behaved as if she were in at a kill.

"Oh my dear" Mrs Weatherby groaned rising majestically from her place.

This movement repeated a thousand thousand times on every side brought each one of those present to his or her feet, except at Philip's table where they sat on transfixed in their moment and Miss Winder's exuberance. Mr Pomfret stood up also. As Jane began to make her way towards Mary he followed and the guests started clapping.

A naturally graceful woman Mrs Weatherby was superb

while she crossed the room afloat between one tall mirror and the other, a look of infinite humility on her proud features. The occasion's shock and excitement had raised her complexion to an even brighter glow, a magnificent effulgence of what all felt she must feel at this promise of grandsons and, at that, from the daughter of what most of them knew to be an old flame with whom she had continued the best of old friends.

Tears stood in many eyes. Some men even cheered discreetly.

And when Jane came to their table she folded Mary Pomfret into so wonderful an embrace while the child half rose from her chair to greet it that not only was the girl's hair not touched or disarranged in this envelopment, but as Mrs Weatherby took the young lady to her heart it must have seemed to most the finest thing they had ever seen, the epitome of how such moments should be, perfection in other words, the acme of manners, and memorable as being the flower, the blossoming of grace and their generation's ultimate instinct of how one should ideally behave.

Mr Pomfret pumped Philip's hand.

Jane was whispering to Mary, "Oh aren't you clever not to have said a word, you clever darling."

One or two of the male guests called for a speech.

Mrs Weatherby disengaged herself with infinite gentleness, held her future daughter-in-law at arm's length as a judge holds a prize lily at the show, then turned to Philip. She leant forward offering a cheek. When he pecked this once, she did not push it smartly back at him. She held firm while John kissed his daughter on the chin. Next she linked arms with both the intended while Mr Pomfret hung at the edge. A fresh storm of clapping greeted this group and now most of the men called for a speech.

Mrs Weatherby nodded like royalty right and left. She wore what might have been called a brave little smile.

But once the appeals for her to say a few words with many a "yes do darling" from the ladies, the moment this clamour grew too insistent Jane whispered to Philip and, with an arm still under Mary's she walked through the uproar back to her table. Philip and John followed, each with a chair. It was noticeable how frightened the girl looked, as was perhaps only natural.

Liz kissed the four of them in turn, the applause rose to a crescendo, and the family group, if Miss Jennings could be said to be of the family, sat down. Once they were all seated it was seen that Richard Abbot had effaced himself, had joined Elaine Winder and her young man at their table where, however, he was now without a chair. This a wine waiter fetched him.

John was first to speak.

"Champagne" he cried to another servant. "We must all have a toast."

"My dear the bill!" Jane said in a low voice.

"Oh will you ever forgive us?" his daughter tremulously asked.

"This is on me" Mr Pomfret explained. "Bring the champagne glasses back" he ordered. "Order another dozen bottles. We shall have to toast 'em" he shouted to the room. Cries of "Good old John" greeted his yell. One of the male guests, rather drunk, seemed about to become dazed.

"Oh my God where's Richard?" Mrs Weatherby demanded in the same low tones.

"He's sat himself down at our table Mamma."

"I still feel quite faint, John."

"You'll be right as a trivet Jane when you've some more wine" Mr Pomfret reassured. "You'll see if you aren't."

"But oh my dear aren't toasts unlucky?"

"Well my boy your mother's a bit bowled over. Ah here we are, and fill them up. All round the room, mind! Now haven't you been a minx keeping this to yourself" he said to his daughter.

"Oh I did worry" she cried to Jane. "But you see it was Philip's twenty firster and people marry younger these days you know, if you see what I mean?"

Mr Pomfret rose to his feet.

"I'm going to ask you all to rise, be upstanding, and to – ah – lift your glasses and drink to – ah – the happy couple." Which, when done, set the party off again. And such a number of people came up to their table to offer congratulations, to twit Jane with not having dropped the least hint, to kiss Mary and to slap John on the back, that it was not for some time later they were able to have private conversation.

WHEN THEY DID find themselves alone once more at this table, John Pomfret incoherently took control,

"Well what's it to be?" he cried to the four of them "a white wedding Mary my love with the old organ and a choir of course?"

"We hadn't got that far yet Daddy."

"But when, how soon? Now you know the party we were to have, you remember I told you Jane, we'll make that into an engagement one, cocktails or something with the few intimate friends to stay over to dinner?"

"How wonderful for you both" Liz cried. "What a bewitching minute this is!"

Jane smiled a trifle sadly, gazed at each in turn. "Isn't it?" she agreed with Miss Jennings. "So much in the one wonderful evening. Oh dear very soon I really quite simply believe I shall have to go home to my bed."

"Jane you'll do nothing of the kind" John Pomfret insisted. "Besides we none of us work tomorrow, we can lie in all day if we wish. It is a terrific occasion! I've been wondering the whole of my life what this moment would be like."

"Dear boy" Mrs Weatherby said to Philip but in tragic tones as she laid a white hand on his arm "if you only knew how your poor mother had dreamed and prayed, yes prayed!"

"But where are you proposing to set up house?" John demanded.

"We haven't actually discussed that have we Philip?" The young man did not answer, moistened his lips with a tongue.

"When I went to see Arthur Morris he told me once he was out of the clinic the doctors had advised him to get away in the country. So his flat at least will be on the market" Miss Jennings suggested.

"Good Lord Liz poor old Arthur has three whole rooms. They'd never be able to afford it."

"The sweet things mustn't start life in too big a little way" Mrs Weatherby approved. She gave her son's arm a squeeze. The young couple frowned what could have been a warning at one another.

"Bless me I don't know when anything ever before in all my time has given me such a crazy lift," the father exclaimed. "Who's to be best man Philip?"

"I couldn't say I'm sure."

"And the bridesmaids Mary?" John Pomfret insisted. "We'll have to be very careful there you know. Of course Liz here must be chief one. You'll do that won't you Liz?"

"Oh John dear you are sweet but you should be serious once in a while" Mrs Weatherby interrupted dolefully and fast. "He simply doesn't understand about these things" she explained to Miss Jennings then seemed to catch herself up. "Oh goodness listen to me" she laughed "the interfering mother-in-law just like you hear about all the time! No John the darlings will have to settle that for themselves."

"I'm too old" Miss Jennings wailed. "Besides poor Liz's been bridesmaid so often. And I always seem to bring such rotten bad luck. They invariably divorce after I've been in the aisle."

"But now we are on the subject" Jane announced "Philip I'm certain your father would've liked you to hold the wedding under our rose window, darling, if he were alive. I know we have practically no connection with the village now but in a way it's still our very own precious church. I shall be buried outside under the yew by his side, I've put that in my little will." She brushed at her eyes with a handkerchief.

"Now Jane" Mr Pomfret expostulated, "this is no time to speak of mourning, top hats and side bands. What next good God? But where are you choosing for the honeymoon?"

"We hadn't quite got round to that yet either" Mary answered.

"Well you haven't thought of much then have you?" he said.

"Really John" Liz exclaimed. "When you're in love you can't make plans about one's plans." She drank another full glass down.

"I don't know when else you plot things out" he replied in obvious delight.

"John" Mrs Weatherby cried. "You're a changed creature! I hardly think that's quite nice do you darling?" and she turned to Liz.

"He's so thrilled" Miss Jennings explained.

"No but to talk of children, nurseries and so on at such a moment, – why my dear you'll be positively indecent in a second!"

Philip Weatherby stifled a yawn.

"Who said a word about nasty sprawling brawling brats Jane?" John Pomfret demanded.

"You did my dear" she said in a dry voice. "Not more than a minute ago. Didn't he darling?" she asked of Liz.

"It's all sho wonderful I don't know whether I'm on my head or my toesh" this lady explained.

"All right then we'll hold a ball, a dance."

"John there's so much to discuss" Jane said.

"I realise you'll say I'm crazy me dear" Mr Pomfret said to his daughter "but ever since you were grown up I've wondered what it would be like talking over marriage settlements with a middle-aged stranger and as I've often told you there's so little in the old kitty that I thought I'd have to take your future father-in-law out and make him drunk. And now good Lord it's going to be Jane that I've known all me life. I can't get over it."

"John do behave yourself" Mrs Weatherby sadly smiled.

"Well we shall be bound to have a chat one of these days won't we Jane?" he demanded.

"I expect you'll know where to find me" she replied and Miss Jennings winced, only she did so very slowly.

"But we shan't want any money" Miss Pomfret claimed with a weak show of determination.

"Nonsense monkey everybody does" her father said.

"Then hadn't you better discuss it with me?" Mr Weatherby asked.

"Philip darling do think before you speak like that" Jane cried.

"Well but you're a woman after all Mamma."

"And I should hope so too indeed. No but your Daddy and I will have to have a little talk shan't we you angelic creature" his mother proposed to Mary with some firmness.

"Of course Mrs Weatherby. I'm sure Philip never meant . . ."

"Now who are you 'Mrs Weatherbying' dear. And you're never to call me 'mother' because I would simply rather die that's all" she laughed. "You do agree with me don't you Liz? John you'd never like Philip to call you Father?"

Mr Weatherby began to show signs of distress. Before he could open his mouth Jane went on rather fast and anxiously.

"No it's all Christian names these days isn't that so, and very sensibly too in my opinion. Anything to do away with the gulf between generations. Oh whenever will these sweet tiresome guests of mine drag themselves off to bed at last. John it's been such a day and a half and I'm so tired!"

"Bed? You think of bed on a night like this?"

"I truly am so tired John dear!!"

"Well I feel I could go on somewhere. What d'you say Liz?"

"Can Philip and I drop you back?"

"I can't very well go before the people I've invited can I?" Mrs Weatherby answered Mary in a sharp tone of voice. "Oh do you think I could send for the bill?"

"Really Jane" Mr Pomfret protested. "You'd never hear the last if you did."

She looked round the noisy party, the people who went from table to table with laughing flushed faces.

"They wouldn't notice you'd hardly think?" she hazarded.

"Shall I get hold of Richard?" Miss Jennings volunteered.

"Perhaps he could go tactfully round Liz to drop a word here and there but not so much that anyone would actually realise."

"No no both of you" John said. "Jane can't break up her own party."

"I don't know" Mr Weatherby suggested "but Mary and I don't feel quite as if we wanted to go home yet. And if we went on somewhere it might start the others off."

"Of course you darlings want to be alone. Oh don't I remember! And who wouldn't!! But Richard has most cruelly deserted me all evening."

"I shouldn't wonder he just found he couldn't intrude" John explained.

"Then you maintain I should have gone to that beastly bitch's daughter's table" Liz almost shouted. She seemed to have difficulty focussing her eyes.

"My dear Liz" he replied with gentleness "I regard you almost as one of the family."

"Thanks" she said and appeared to subside. "OK" she said.

"A woman needs another by her at a time like this" Mrs Weatherby murmured.

"Well parents" Philip began. "What say if we simply pushed off?"

"Certainly not" Jane sharply reproved him. "Not now you're the guests of the evening. And before this surprise started it was your twenty firster after all. Please remember, if only to please me please remember that!"

"Why of course" Mary Pomfret agreed and seemed most nervous. "We wouldn't dream of the slightest thing . . ."

"Hm . . . m" Mrs Weatherby replied. "That's settled then."

"You know Mary" her father pronounced "this is a great moment in a woman's life. You must be extra nice with Jane, it has quite bowled her over."

"But I am Daddy."

"Of course you are you angel" the older woman agreed. "Now John don't butt in between, we shall manage our own affairs perfectly shan't we dear? Still I can't tell why all these people shouldn't go. I really feel I almost hardly know them now. I'm so tired don't you understand John? No of course you two must stay at least for the present, dreadfully dull as it must be for you both. I've such a tearing headache. God what a day!"

"Anything I can do Mamma?"

"Just don't let poor darling Penelope the little saint into this secret, promise me will you? I know her better than anyone in the whole wide world but even I couldn't tell what the results might be now, I wouldn't dare."

"I say, she could be one of our bridesmaids" Philip said.

"I should hope so indeed" his mother took him up. "If not then I can't possibly imagine who else. And when we've just got her over the man in chains down at Brighton! Oh my dear if you didn't ask the child why she'd simply rather die."

"Well it's not exactly secret now is it Mamma?"

"But we must break it gently don't you understand" his mother answered. "We've had this wedding trouble before with the sainted little sweet. Oh I blame myself but really

John wasn't it wicked of you and now only four months later we're to go through this all over again! And when I told her the facts of life a year back, she was just five and a half then, will you believe me but she's forgotten every word, she must have done from what the little angel's said lately. Oh isn't parenthood confusing! I always tell these girls when they get engaged they simply can't guess what they're in for." At which she gaily laughed "Now there I go again" she went on, beaming at Mary "I do declare I'd quite forgotten for the second! What will you think of me? Oh Philip your stupid Mamma!"

"When they began giving sex instruction at Council schools" Philip told them "there was a woman wrote to say the lesson had taken ninety minutes each week off her daughter's mathematics and surely maths must be more important."

"My dear boy" Mrs Weatherby approved "that was almost witty."

"Good for you Philip!" Mr Pomfret said. "Well then mum's the word where Pen's concerned eh?"

"Yes, you must all and every one of you promise faithfully" Jane agreed. "In fact the less spoken about this secret engagement the better, so it doesn't get to her sacred little ears poor soul."

LATER ON, when John Pomfret's excitement drove him to circulate among the other tables with Liz and Mary in tow, Richard Abbot came back to his rightful place at Jane's left hand.

"Where have you been?" the lady cried "and what d'you mean by it just when I wanted you!"

"Family matter I thought. Felt an outsider!"

"Well Liz didn't did she? She stayed. Oh Richard you do let me down at times of crisis."

"Now my dear this's been a great day for all. Only natural to be overwrought a bit."

"Oh I am" she wailed, her large eyes even more enormous. "Don't you think Richard you could persuade them to go so I can get home to bed?"

"My dear Jane, can't do that! Let me fetch you a black coffee."

"In a moment. No, sit here" and she patted the chair next her. "Oh Richard I'm worried about little Penelope. You remember how she was after she imagined she'd married John? Well what will it be like when she realises her brother has got engaged to what she must truly believe to be her own stepdaughter, have you thought of that?"

"She'll have forgotten everything about it."

"But how can she I ask you? Richard do concentrate, this is important to me. Her little sanity's at stake."

"She'll have forgotten about that tomfoolery with John I meant."

"If you say so, then you pit yourself against the psychoanalyst. I asked Maud Winder's advice who'd such a lot of trouble with her girl at one time and I went to the best. He told me it might have bruised Pen's soul, he couldn't be sure he said until he had seen the child but I wouldn't allow that, don't you think I was right, I mean one never knows where these clever famous men will end does one, playing politics with my own precious darling's very being, Richard?"

"Don't hold with 'em myself."

"Yet I'm not trying to say the chief responsibility doesn't rest with me, it must of course, it always will, oh my dear the load devilish Providence has put on my poor bended back! No I have to guard her against her sweet self. And when she hears and starts one of her things the desperate brave little martyr, I shan't be able to turn everything off as I did to finish the escapist at Brighton by giving the child a bag she liked to hang from the elbow she would insist on holding. Still if I have to I shall think of a ruse, it's what I'm here for after all. But the strain Richard!"

"Shouldn't wonder if Philip's a bit worked up too eh?"

"Oh the boy's all right. Not normal of course but in absolutely no need of help I can tell you."

"Don't know Jane. Big moment in a young fellow's life, must be."

"How can you judge? You yourself have simply never even risked it."

"Not from want of trying."

"My dear how utterly sweet you can be!" she said. "In spite of this deplorable habit of yours of not being there when you're wanted. But don't you see Richard you're older, tougher. Oh dear have I been horrible, torturing you all this time?"

"If I were you I'd decide Penelope was all right for the moment and concentrate a bit on Philip."

"How can I make up my mind against my better judgement?"

"Then there's Mary to consider" he reminded Mrs Weatherby. "Tricky few days this in a girl's life, always will be. She'll need making a fuss over."

"Does one never have a rest?"

"You ought to have a man about to take some of the load off your shoulders."

"To put a greater weight on, you mean! Oh I didn't intend to be beastly, you must believe. But I'm at my wit's end Richard."

LATER STILL Philip and Mary made good their escape, got away to a nightclub.

"Well" he said "I told you! It went quite all right."

"Oh Philip darling" she cried above but somehow under the music so that she sounded hoarse "they'll never let us marry, I know they won't, isn't it awful!"

"But see here" he objected "everything worked like a dream. I swear this was the only way to deal with my mother. I learned by watching Pen as a matter of fact. When she wants whatever it may be she just takes it; as soon as she feels ill she doesn't just say she feels something coming on, she is ill and Mamma loves the whole business."

"We should've got married first. There's what we ought to have told them, not that we were only engaged."

"I know but it's so rude to the relations when people elope."

"Yes you're right" she gulped.

"And then eloping's out of date, it went out with horses."

"Oh dear now they're all eaten poor things."

"Too many people on this island keep carnivorous pets Mary" he replied. "The waste is fearful."

"But what happens next Philip?"

"With our parents? Well you know how it is. They'll argue, there'll be no end to the amount they're sure to squawk which they'll love. And Mamma will weep once or twice and your father will act pretty idiotically for quite a time."

"Don't say anything against Daddy darling, please."

"OK then lay off Mamma."

"What d'you mean, I haven't said a word about her!"

"It was just I thought you seemed a bit unenthusiastic when you made out she'd try and stop us."

"I said 'they'. I didn't say anything against her."

"Well who is 'they' in that case?"

"All of them."

"But look here it passed off awfully well didn't it? I mean they seemed overjoyed to me. As a matter of fact I thought my speech went rather grandly didn't you?"

"Oh you were wonderful darling" she warmly assured

him. "Heavens though I do feel I'd been put through a mangle."

"Poor sweet" he said and squeezed the hot hand he was holding. "Shall we dance?"

They danced. Eyes closed, cheek to cheek, better than ever before. When they had had enough for a time they came back to their table.

"That's the way to do the rumba" she told him. "See that man on the left, how he makes the girl go round while he stays in the centre."

"Should I do that with you?"

"Of course darling."

"I doubt if I ever shall be able."

"Then take lessons silly."

"I say" he said "you do feel better now, you must?"

"I think so, yes."

"Can't you find out yes or no."

"But no one can. First something inside says everything is fine" she wailed "and the next moment it tells you that something which overshadows everything else is very bad just like an avalanche!"

"I'm so sorry" he said. "I truly am."

They danced again and again until, as the long night went on they had got into a state of unthinking happiness perhaps.

A WEEK LATER Mrs Weatherby asked John Pomfret to dinner.

"And how is dear Liz?" she enquired as she brought the man a glass of sherry.

"Quite well I trust."

"Aren't you seeing so much of her now then John?"

"But of course" he said. "The fact is this news about our respective children has rather thrown me out of my normal gait."

"So it's become a question of striding between you and Liz" Mrs Weatherby commented. Her look on him over the decanter was one of sweet compassion. "Oh my dear" she continued "you must be careful. Don't let it end as our love did in great country walks."

"Really Jane when do I ever get away?" he cried. "All my work in town here, and now this engagement! Philip and Mary are going to keep us pretty well occupied you know. Lot to arrange and so on."

"I'm sure" she agreed. "Just sit back and relax."

"And how is little Penelope?" he enquired.

She made a beautiful flowing gesture of resignation. "Oh my dear" she said. "Sometimes I bless Providence I have a man like you can share my problems."

"Isn't Richard much use then?"

"I don't know what I should do without him but he has that failing John of the absolutely true, true to one I mean, of being almost completely unimaginative poor dear."

Mr Pomfret laughed. "I see" he said. "Sometimes I have just wondered what you found in Richard."

"Loyalty" she breathed and smoothed her skirts.

"Which you never came across in me?"

"Don't let's rake up the past darling. What's over's over."

"Enough's enough you mean?"

She let out a gentle peal of laughter, leaning back on the sofa.

"Oh John aren't you horrid!" she cried.

"Good sherry you have here" he said.

"I'm so glad you say that. Ned makes me go to his man and I wouldn't know."

"While Maud Winder sends you to her psychologist about Penelope?"

"No but John who told? Oh don't people talk!"

"You yourself did."

"I'd quite forgot. No one must know darling, it would be unfair on my sad longsuffering angel. Who'd want to marry a girl later who'd been analysed?"

"Would it make any difference?"

"Who can tell my dear? It might quite disgust Pen with all that side of life. So you won't breathe a word John will you? Besides I never did let him set his terrible hypnotising eyes on her, no I guard my poppet too well for that. The thing is, she's heard!"

"Heard what?"

"Why that they're secretly engaged."

"There's not so much secret now surely after the public announcement? It must be all over London."

"But we've put no announcement in the Press yet John?"

"That's just one of the matters I wanted to have a word about."

"Yes there's so much to discuss" she sighed.

"Then you don't think Penelope ought to be a bridesmaid? Overexcite her or something?"

"My dear one she'd simply die as things are if Mary didn't ask her. It was Isabella. Penelope absolutely jabbers in Italian now, so wonderful, while I can still hardly put two words together. And you see I don't understand what they say all the time. I spent hours with the dictionary to warn the woman not to breathe a word." Mrs Weatherby merrily laughed. "I must have looked a sight poring over it and in the end perhaps I said the opposite, as one does, even gave her orders to tell Penelope at once. Oh John what it is not to understand a syllable of one's only servant's beastly tongue! But the child knows, she babbles of the wedding all day and I'm afraid for her."

"You know Jane" Mr Pomfret interrupted "I think I'm going to grow very fond of Philip."

"I should hope so too. He's such a splendid bull of a boy."

"I seem to have got really far with him the last few days."

"What d'you talk to him about? My brother-in-law?"

Mr Pomfret appeared to ignore the dryness of her tone. He was peering at the sherry in his glass.

"We shall make friends. I always wanted a son" he said.

"I'd so like to give Mary just a touch of advice about her clothes" Jane suggested in a small voice.

"Then we seem ideally suited as in-laws" Mr Pomfret laughed. "Though you must not mind if the girl has thoughts of her own; she can be very pigheaded about dresses I believe."

"Why how d'you mean John?"

"Liz took her round the various establishments some time back and didn't get her own way much so I understand."

"But isn't that natural? You can hardly say darling Liz has any taste at all."

"I never notice what a woman wears. Liz always looks very nice and neatly turned out to me."

Mrs Weatherby smiled.

"Neat is not quite the word!"

"Well for the matter of that I'd like five minutes with Philip about the cut of his jib."

"He goes to the best tailors."

"It's his hats dear Jane."

"He's never bareheaded is he? I should hate him to be."

"So wide brimmed."

"Now John you're not to put the poor boy into one of those bowler things or I'll never speak to you again."

"Do you notice what men are wearing?"

"Of course."

"Then did I get the suit I have on now from off a hook or was it made for me?"

"You ask me that when you wouldn't know if I was in one of my beloved mother's Ascot dresses this minute!"

"What tailor does Philip patronise?"

"His awful uncle's."

"Well of course I haven't the advantage of knowing your brother-in-law well enough to have been acquainted with his cutter."

"It's Highcliffe I believe, in that little passage off the Arcade."

"Never heard of the man." There was a pause. Then Mr Pomfret went on "What made Philip choose Ned Weatherby's man?"

"Family reasons. Philip feels all men who are closely related should go to the same place for everything."

"That's what must lead one to think he's in livery then."

"But John the boy never wears striped waistcoats."

"We shall have to change all of it Jane. Who d'you say your winemerchant was?"

"Ned's."

"Curious. Remind me to ask you the address some time. So has Philip gone traditional with the tradespeople? Can't say I remember anything of the sort in my family."

"Then you've forgotten your Aunt Eloise."

"What about her?"

"Wasn't it she who insisted on everyone getting everything on the route served by such and such a bus?"

"Extraordinary memory you have Jane. Whenever did I tell you that?"

"On one of those despairingly long walks you took me, dear."

They both laughed. There was a short pause.

"Well I think all this business is rather marvellous" he began again. "It's given me a new lease of life Jane. Takes me back to the days we were walking out! I'm sure I couldn't think of anyone more perfect for Mary than your Philip."

"What a sweet sentimental person you can be" she replied. "I believe most men are."

"No seriously" he said "it's all I could've wished."

"I never imagined, who would, I mean think of you and me sitting here like this after all that's happened, and in a discussion how we're to become related by the back door so to speak!"

"Not at all" he objected. "The main entrance."

"D'you really think so? Don't you find your children, your own girl so remote?"

"Why should I Jane?"

"But Mary's a girl!"

"And what difference does sex bring to the relationship?"

"You see I'm forever making allowances for Philip because he's a man" she explained. "And the more so by reason of my not having a husband any longer of course. It's the same with you John. If you were married now you'd be so greatly critical, no not that, shall I say choosy about Mary."

"Would I?"

"Well I mean about her clothes and everything."

"Why?"

"Because you'd get some advice I suppose. I'm sure I don't know. What d'you expect me to say?"

"I couldn't tell you Jane" he said smiling, and seemed very comfortable in the chair with his sherry.

"I hope Isabella's not to be late again like she was last time, or is each time if I'm not to tell a lie" Mrs Weatherby said. "Supposing I shouted to her in the kitchen?"

"I'm quite all right. Never been more comfortable in my life."

"Well you did arrive a weeny bit early didn't you? The thing is, as I've already explained, ever since she told darling Pen all about the secret engagement I've been terrified to say much to Isabella in case unbeknownst I'm telling the woman the opposite. Never mind, I expect we can wait a bit. Then are you quite easy in your heart of hearts about Mary and Philip?"

"My dear" he said "I can't remember when I've been more pleased."

"It just crossed my mind, only a moment ago to tell the truth, John I have almost wondered and you are the one person in the world to whom I'd bring myself to mention this, but don't you feel they both might be rather young?"

"Young? My dear girl what age were you when you married?"

"Eighteen months younger than your lovely Mary I know, oh I know!" she cried. "Still wouldn't you agree we were different then?"

"Different? In what way?" An edge had come onto his voice.

"It's so difficult to look back to those golden wonderful days" she moaned, "to feel back to how we felt then! I don't know but I sometimes think I was simply insane marrying when I did so I missed all my fun."

"Nonsense my dear" Mr Pomfret said firmly. "You never lived until you met me and that was years later."

"Oh why didn't I wait?" she murmured gently with a brilliant flattering smile full on him. "That was when I made the greatest mistake. And how about you? What d'you think?"

"Me? Oh I've been an absolute fool all me life."

"There's not many would say that about you John. But, if we were complete idiots is there any reason why we should let the children fall into the selfsame trap?"

"Yes Jane and who's to stop 'em?"

"Ah" she said "ah! Yet these runaway affairs?" she hazarded.

"That's what I like about our two. They haven't eloped."

"Not yet, sweet Providence forbid!"

107

"My dear" he remonstrated. "I say nothing against Mary when I tell you she is far too level headed. And Philip would be frightened of what his uncle's tradesmen might find to say."

She narrowed her great eyes.

"John" she warned him "that's not funny!"

"Have I said something?" he exclaimed with what seemed to be genuine innocence. "Look here I do apologise. Now that the children have got engaged I suppose I'm wallowing in intimacy, there you are, thinking out aloud no end of ill-considered things. There's been so little time to adjust oneself has there?"

"No no" she agreed "I was only absurd for a minute and ridiculously touchy. Forgive me dear John! Oh yes it has all been hasty quick hasn't it?"

"Then you really think they're too young though you admit there's very little we can do and that we married younger?"

"But John we had money. It didn't have to be love in a cottage for us."

"Quite out of date nowadays" he laughed. "Most expensive things in the world, cottages! It's the old garret for the nonce all right."

"And can you see Philip in one?"

"No Jane to tell the honest truth I can't, yet that's Mary's affair I suppose? And then I imagine you and I'll be able to help a little."

Mrs Weatherby covered her face with her fat white fingers in rings.

"Oh there you go" she moaned "and I've been dreading it all evening! I shall have to see Mr Thicknesse which I do terribly tremble at always!! I'm such an absolute fool over money matters John!"

"Thicknesse the family Oliver Twist?"

"Yes the lawyer. You remember him" she said, still from behind her hands but in a stronger tone.

"Never had dealings with the man myself."

"But you did. When we were wickedly threatened with cross divorces." Her voice dropped to a whisper. "Don't tell me you've forgotten even that?"

"Oh old Thicknesse" he cried cheerfully. "Yes I've got him now right enough. Lord I'm sorry for anyone who has to call on that fellow! And you say he's still alive when a fine chap thirty years younger like poor old Arthur Morris lies dying in bed?"

"No don't" she wailed. "No one, simply no one is to mention Arthur again in my presence! I told Penelope. I forbad her."

"Yes I expect you'll have to call on Master Thicknesse. Unless you'd rather I went?"

"Oh well wouldn't that look rather queer?" she cried, lowered the hands from her face and looked at Mr Pomfret with a tiny smile at the corners of those magnificent eyes. "Besides I'm afraid it may turn out to be quite like those Egyptian tombs they're always finding and are so proud of, quite empty, robbed."

"You mean the sly old devil's got away with some?"

"Mr Thicknesse?" she gasped and actually glanced over a shoulder. "Hush my dear, do think what you're saying!"

John roared with laughter, put his drink down, even leaned right back to let himself go. She caught the infection, or seemed to, and soon in her turn was dabbing at her eyes.

"Darling" he brought out at last, a few tears about his cheekbones "you're wonderful! I don't know what I'd do without you!"

Mrs Weatherby stopped laughing at once.

"You've managed without someone an unconscionably long time John."

"Dear where do you get these long words suddenly?"

"My old governess" she replied in a tart voice. "What were we talking about?"

"Lord knows" he said. "That's the effect you have on me. I forget time and place."

"Then I don't" she gaily laughed. "And I think I know what it may be. Isabella must have misunderstood again and is waiting for us in the dining room. Let's go along, shall we, if only to try, anyway?"

JOHN POMFRET invited Mr Abbot to have a bite to eat with him at the Club.

"I asked you to drop over because I'm worried in my mind to do with this business about my Mary" he told Richard.

"Young love not running smooth eh?"

"I shouldn't say that for the simple reason I've no means of finding out. They look happy enough bless 'em but they don't let on much. Tell you the truth I wanted to enlist your help with Jane."

"You've known her longest, John."

"I'd like to put the whole thing before you. Basically I think a man's no right to stand between his child and her happiness." He laughed. "Lord that sounds a pompous pronouncement but you follow what I mean? And it's damned hard to get down to arrangements with someone like Jane you've known all your life."

"Expect it may be" Mr Abbot agreed.

"Good, I thought you'd catch on. The fact is I've been uncommonly careful not to rush Jane in any shape or form and then this week the summons I'd been awaiting came and she asked me round to dinner. Well we did have a bit of a chat while that Italian woman of hers kept us hanging on for the meal but I can't say we got anywhere. After we'd sat down to eat and later back in her room again it was hardly mentioned; to tell the truth we got laughing over old days and there you are."

"Wonderful food Jane gives one. Can't imagine how she does it these days."

Mr Pomfret turned on Richard Abbot a long considering look.

"Food's not been too bad in the Club lately" he said at last. "Richard are you with me about all this?"

"Completely ignorant of the whole issue" Mr Abbot answered.

"Well I can't promise there is an issue" John pointed out. "Only perhaps that Jane doesn't seem wildly keen on the engagement. It's not so much what she puts into words as everything she doesn't mention and for somebody who's never been exactly silent all her life that may or may not be significant. How do you weigh things up?"

"She might be a trifle upset about Penelope?"

"I know but don't you think Pen's often a blind, Richard? Doesn't Jane use the child as a shield?"

"She has no need that I can see."

"Of course not" Mr Pomfret concurred. "Never met anyone better able to look after herself than Jane."

"Wonderful manager. Marvellous party she gave!"

"Superb! A trifle unfortunate though the way the children brought their marriage in."

"As a matter of fact I a bit felt that" Mr Abbot agreed. "When all's said and done it was Jane's show. Speaking as Philip did he stole the thunder considerably or so I fancied."

"Wasn't it his twenty firster?"

"May have been" Richard Abbot admitted. "But a mother has the right to celebrate having raised her own son to man's estate surely?"

"Admitted" John allowed him. "All the same we celebrated by ourselves didn't we when you and I ceased to be minors?"

"No doubt Philip did so."

"I fancy they're a bit short, wouldn't run to two entertainments. Who could these days?"

"Don't know at all. None of my business John."

There was another pause while Mr Pomfret studied Richard Abbot.

"D'you like Mary?" he asked at last. "Forget I'm her father. Well of course you can't. But tell me what I ought to do. They seem very much in love. I don't say I've been particularly keen on Philip in the past but Mary's chosen and that's enough for me. Besides, now I've seen a bit more of him as one does on these occasions I find there's a lot in the boy. I'm not saying a word against Jane mind but he's missed having a man about the house. Have you run across him in one of his hats?"

"Bloody terrible. Don't speak of 'em."

"Aren't they?" Mr Pomfret agreed in a relieved sort of voice. "Later on I may be able to manage something about it. But are you on my side about those two or aren't you?"

"Not for me to take sides. You know Jane better than me John. Comparative newcomer is all I am."

"You'll excuse my saying this but you aren't. Why I hardly ever see old Jane now, and then only at the cost of a row each time with Liz. No, all I want is the children's happiness and how to get it, that's what I'm after."

"Won't they marry in spite of anything either of you may say?" Mr Abbot asked.

"Of course Richard. Simply I'd like to avoid the sort of unpleasantness which could follow, shortage of cash, no help from Jane because she's been rushed or feels hurt, the hundred and one things to dog them once they're back from the honeymoon."

"Don't ask me how Jane's fixed for money."

"Which is not the point with great respect old man. There's every kind of support Jane can bring if she wishes. But look here if she didn't agree" Mr Pomfret pointed out "matters might go sour, all sorts of awful things, trouble and so on. Oh we shall be out of it right enough, you and I. I'm thinking of Mary."

"Grandchildren do the trick d'you consider?"

"Well naturally. Still supposing there aren't any at first. And how can anyone carry it off in a single room, if they have to live in the beginning with practically no more than a single room, and on what they earn?"

"As I know Jane she'd never resist a baby" Mr Abbot said.

"But good God Richard have they to breed like rabbits to get recognition?"

"They've always got you haven't they?"

"What's the use? I've no money left! Who has?"

"Well thank God I'm not in your shoes."

"It's not as bad as that is it Richard? D'you mean you think Jane actually opposes the idea?"

"Me? How should I know? She doesn't discuss anything with me, good God no. Damned if I can say what I'd advise."

"You don't sound very cheerful old man I must say."

"It's like this John" Mr Abbot explained "and by the way I wouldn't care for anyone to know what I'm going to tell you now. The fact is Jane and I may see a bit of one another from time to time but she doesn't confide in me, never has. Damned self-reliant woman in my opinion Jane and always was."

"I don't know I ever found her any different" Mr Pomfret agreed. "So you can't say what she's driving at?"

Richard Abbot considered his host in a long expressionless stare.

"D'you suppose Jane knows herself?" he asked in the end. "Probably got a violent sensationalism over this marriage business. Expect she'll hide it under sweetness and light if you follow me. Then when she's ready" and Mr Abbot jerked his hands up from his knees "out it will all come. Just like that."

"Oh my God you appal me" John Pomfret cried with signs of agitation.

"Could go either way with her, for or against" said Richard in what seemed to be great satisfaction. Upon which Mr Pomfret took his guest to the bar, they fell in with friends and dined in a party. No more was said of the engagement that night.

MR WEATHERBY and Miss Pomfret were in the saloon bar of the public house they used in Knightsbridge. Their becoming engaged to be married had not made the smallest difference in either's manner or appearance. As usual they sat over two light ales and, when they talked, spoke for a time almost in asides to one another.

"You know my blue hat darling?" she asked.

"Which one?" he vaguely said.

Mary gave a short technical description.

"Well I might" he admitted but did not seem as if he could.

"Your mother doesn't like it."

"I don't know that I care for many of hers."

"D'you think I dress horribly badly darling?"

"Why Mary you must be sure I don't."

"Because you see I'm wearing everything I've got for you now darling or almost, and I'd like to get some idea of what you feel suits me if we are to buy all these clothes."

"What clothes?"

"Frocks. Dresses. Trousseau. Getting married you know."

"Sorry darling. I've never done this sort of thing before. I wasn't thinking."

"Nor me! The trouble is Philip these older women have and do, they've got us at a disadvantage."

"Your father doesn't like my headgear either."

"Daddy? He's never said a word."

"He has to me."

"How did he object?"

"Artistic was the word he used."

"Oh dear I'm really sorry darling because I always think Daddy's the best dressed man I meet, of his own generation of course."

"Well I rather fancy the way Mamma gets herself up sometimes."

Miss Pomfret laughed.

"I'll tell you what" she said. "This conversation's becoming almost barbed isn't it?"

He gave a wry smile. "Might be" he agreed.

She took his hand under the table, stroked the ring finger with her thumb. A silence drew across them.

She watched a couple up at the bar with a miniature poodle on a stool in between. Its politeness and general agitation appeared half human. But when a man came in with a vast brindled bull terrier on a lead as thick as an ox's tail the smaller dog turned her back to the drinks, ignored her owners at once, and gazed at the killer with thrilled lack lustre eyes. For his part the bull terrier lay down as soon as the man on the other end of his lead let him, and, with an air of acute embarrassment gazed hard at the poodle, then away again, then, as though he could not help it, back once more. He started to whine. Miss Pomfret smiled. The other occupants began paying attention to these interested animals.

"Rather sweet isn't he?" she said.

"Who? Your father?"

"Oh no, Daddy always is. The bull terrier I mean."

"So long as he doesn't take it into his head to murder that other wretched brute in front of our very eyes."

"But he won't Philip. She's a lady."

"I've known it happen."

"The man who's with him's got him safe."

"They'll do something crazy to let them meet before the evening's out. We'll see blood spilt yet" he opined.

"Philip darling do you like dogs?" she enquired.

"I do and I don't" he said.

"Because I was thinking when we were married I'd rather love to have one for my own."

"Might be a bit awkward if we both went out every day to work."

"Oh I expect the landlady would look after things."

"I wonder" he said.

She dropped his hand.

"You're in rather a filthy mood this evening" she remarked.

He drew himself up to finish his glass of beer.

"I'm sorry Mary" he said and appeared to be so. "I say I saw Uncle Ned at tea today."

"What, did he come round?"

"To Mamma's? Good Lord no. I went to him."

"Was he pleased about us?"

"D'you know I didn't dare tell."

"Not dare tell him!" she echoed. "That's not very nice to me, now then!"

"Oh it wasn't that. It simply seems he detests Mamma and won't have her mentioned in his presence hardly. Seemed very surprised when I sent up my name. Even told me he'd been in two minds whether to say he was at home. Me, his own nephew!"

She laughed. "But perhaps he was busy darling."

"No Mary it's no laughing matter. And when I can't remember ever having met the man. You'd think he'd have some family sense! And then when he started on Mamma like that!"

"Oh I am so sorry Philip. What on earth did he say?"

"Nothing much actually. I came away with the idea he really must be rather mad. In fact of course I had to stand up for her and so on. But that it should happen at a time like this, with marriage on our hands! After all a wedding is a family affair isn't it?"

"Of course darling" she agreed with every appearance of concern, took his hand back in her own under the table

116

and began to squeeze it hard. "Oh dear you mustn't get upset."

"It all came as a bit of a shock" he said in a calm voice.

"But Philip you'd seen him before?"

"Never that I remember."

"And there was Daddy telling me you went to your Uncle Ned's tailor."

"Well I do."

"Then you must have met Uncle first for him to recommend you."

"Mamma gave me the name. My father went there too."

"Oh of course darling. How silly of me!"

"What on earth was your parent doing to talk about my tailor?"

"Oh nothing really."

"Doesn't he like the suits I wear either?" the young man asked.

"You mustn't bother about Daddy darling. He's tremendously of his own generation can't you see? I expect in their day it was only possible for them to get their clothes from the one man."

"But my father went to Highcliffe too."

"Of course he did. I'll tell you what" she announced. "The next time I think of it I'll ask Daddy what he really meant."

"And you might get him to give you the address of his tailor."

"Oh Philip darling shall I really?"

"I've been rather disappointed in Uncle Ned" the young man said. "I don't see why I should favour his tradespeople any longer."

A DAY OR TWO LATER, in what for once was brilliant sunshine, Mary Pomfret and Philip Weatherby were sitting on a Sunday afternoon in Hyde Park.

"D'you mind what part of London we live in?" she asked.

"Wherever you like" he said.

She frowned. "That's not quite what I meant" she pointed out. "If you had your dearest wish just which district would you prefer?"

"I don't mind" he replied.

"Because darling I think we ought to start looking about you know?"

"I leave it to you" he said, his eyes out over the Serpentine as a dog swam to a thrown branch in the foreground. "I shan't interfere. A home's a woman's business."

"But Philip before I begin to search I shall have to know what we can afford."

"I'll hand over my salary every week less ten cigarettes a day. I've decided to give up beer. If we like to go to the pub you can take me on the housekeeping money."

"Oh darling aren't you making it all sound rather grim?"

"I think marriage is. We'll have a lot of responsibilities."

"Philip don't you want to marry me?"

At that he turned and took her hand. He did not say anything but there must have been something in his eyes or expression for she sighed as though satisfied.

"Oh darling" she said. "You had me quite worried for a moment."

They sat on in silence for a while. He gazed at his feet. She searched every cranny of his face with her eyes.

"Because I don't think we need be right down to the bone" she began again. "I mean Daddy's said he'd be able to help a bit."

"D'you believe one ought to accept anything from one's parents Mary?"

"They haven't much I know, that is compared with what they were once accustomed to" she said. "And yet what they've been allowed to keep is family cash isn't it? Savings handed down from father to son?"

As she put this forward she allowed a small smile to play almost imperceptibly about the corners of her mouth.

"That's a sound point certainly" he replied. Then he stopped. He did open his lips once more after a minute but relapsed into silence instead. She waited. At last he went on,

"As a matter of fact Mamma has been to see the dread Mr Thicknesse." He laughed. "You don't know who he is now, do you?"

"Of course" she gaily answered. "Your family lawyer."

"How did you find out?" he demanded and looked sternly at her again. Meeting his eyes she stuck her chin up in rather an attractive manner.

"Daddy told me!"

"You discuss quite a lot with your Father don't you?"

"If you talked over things more with me I mightn't have to."

There was a silence.

"Oh Philip don't be so absurd. You're forever speaking about the family though I notice you don't ever seem to mention we might have children of our own, and now you object to my going into things with my Father. I think you're beastly."

"I'm sorry" he said "darling truly I am" and took her hand once more. "The fact is I get worried. You were dead right just now when you pointed out people of our parents' age had the experience over us. You see I'm not sure it's right to accept money from them."

"But your father may have left you some Philip."

"Oh if he had they'd tell me. They could hardly not could they?"

"Still why don't you go and see Mr Thicknesse?"

"Me?" he echoed. "But Mamma's been."

"I see" she said in an unseeing voice.

"It won't be a great deal cheaper for her with me gone" he went on. "There's Penelope to consider. I mean I don't see how we can afford Arthur Morris' flat do you? Three whole rooms!"

"We might have to if we had children."

"Oh I don't suppose it will ever fall vacant" he answered. When she did not say anything he continued,

"As to the little Weatherbys they'll have to wait till they arrive."

She gasped and then she laughed.

"Little Weatherbys" she cried. "How extraordinary! All this time I've been thinking of them as little Pomfrets. Darling Philip I am absurd. I never even imagined I'd have to change my name!"

"Well that's the idea isn't it?" he said.

"Then if I must I'd like to sooner rather than later darling."

"Whenever you say" he said.

She frowned and bit her lip.

A FEW DAYS afterwards Mrs Weatherby had John Pomfret to dinner alone for the second time since their respective children had become engaged.

The meal was announced almost before his sherry was poured and now he found himself seated by candle light in front of some fried veal and unable as yet to start discussing arrangements.

"My dear" he broke in as soon as he decently could "I'm very flattered. Here I am enjoying the most delicious dinner. But we have a lot to go over. Time is never short I know.

All the same I should be glad to get down to things."

"Darling John you were always so tempestuous."

"Thank you Jane. I don't know that I usually let the grass grow under my feet. But this has to do with Mary's happiness."

"Well then I went to see Mr Thicknesse like I promised."

"And what did the old fool say?"

"Oh my dear" Mrs Weatherby began as though a roll of drums had preluded a performance which was late only owing to the negligence of the conductor out of sight in the prompter's box "it was terrible, I never thought I should survive. You know he always seemed to take such a curious view in the old days about our case John. I'm sure if they had ever come to court I'd've had more real true sympathy from the judge, although we were paying Mr Thicknesse weren't we?"

"Damned expensive he was into the bargain."

"Well I went" she repeated. "When I got back I had to take one of my little tablets and lie down. It's really too bad Philip is so young and can't help out with these business things. As for you John dear Mr Thicknesse's manner to me was so strange once you might almost have knocked him down if you'd been there. Oh how does one change one's lawyer?"

"Simply by leaving him."

"Leave Mr Thicknesse, I'd never dare! After all I've been through with him! But do you know I can't understand a word he says."

"Hasn't he a clerk then?"

"Oh yes. A young one. He's sweet. He'd do anything for me. When I've something very urgent and I get on the telephone they put me through sometimes to Mr Eustace. Isn't it a queer name? I suppose that's only when the old devil of a man is engaged. Really isn't one's life too awful, to be at the mercy of men like Mr Thicknesse!"

"Don't beat about the bush Jane."

"It's simply I can't be hurried. John do be sensible dear. I won't be rushed, just won't."

She left her veal, went over to the sideboard and fetched a china dish of chocolates across to Mr Pomfret.

"Beautiful bit of meat you have here" he said.

"It's always such a pleasure to entertain you John" she replied. "No but I mean what can all the hurry be?" she went on. "Only three weeks ago when they so startled us all and now their whole lives in front of them!"

"You do feel they're too young?"

"I may have done at first but it was you, surely, confounded us both with my own marriage as though you were prosecuting me darling. We went to Folkestone for the first night of the honeymoon." She sighed. "My beloved mother sent her maid until we crossed to France next morning and the woman got so excited when she unpacked for me I couldn't get rid of her, so awkward. No I don't say they're over young now though Philip of course has a lot still to learn, not too young exactly, but where's the violent haste in all this John dear?"

"Oh none. But before there may be there's so much to discuss."

"You don't mean . . . ?"

"Of course not Jane. Only engagements often end in a race. Nerves turn ragged."

"All right but don't you get cross!"

"Jane darling I'm not. Of course we must take our time."

"That's much better" she said, giving him her great smile. "Because I think Mary's the sweetest child in the whole world. So lucky for dear Philip. But we must be practical. After all we are their parents. Oh who would've ever imagined darling us sitting opposite each other like we are solemnly eating our dinners with the children's marriage to decide!"

"It's a sobering thought certainly."

"Aren't you pleased then?" she asked.

"It makes me feel so old" he replied in a bantering tone of voice but with evident caution. "Something like this can happen before one is ready for it."

"Then you do think they're rather babies?"

"No no" he said quickly. "What I meant was I'm the one who's too young. And I know you are."

She laughed. "One can forever be certain you'll make delicious fun out of serious moments and I love you for it darling. Though I don't say I did always."

"We never made a joke of our affairs in the old days. It might've been better if we had."

"How d'you mean?" she demanded sharply.

"Well we were very very serious weren't we?"

"I should hope so too" she said.

"It was most painful at the time though."

"Oh I thought I would die" she sighed.

"And did we get anywhere by waiting Jane?"

"No don't" she moaned. "We must simply never go over all that again."

"It's a thought what I've just said just the same."

"Oh dear I sometimes feel men must be wildly insensitive. If I knew enough of the language I'd ask Isabella if it's like this in Italy."

"You wouldn't want a fat man about the house always singing opera."

"I might be able to put up with it."

"Now Jane you know how quick-tempered you can be, particularly when you've those headaches of yours and won't stand any noise."

"I'm not like that now" she answered. "But we mustn't talk over ourselves and the old days tragically sweet as they were. We're here to be practical and I think we have been John."

"Well well" he said with an edge of sarcasm on his voice.

"My dear what's the matter with you now?" she asked at once. "I thought I was being exactly as you wished."

He laughed. "You're too much for me Jane" he admitted.

"And just don't you forget it" she replied, once more beaming upon him.

Upon which she changed the conversation and in spite of one or two halfhearted efforts on his part he was unable to discuss the children further that evening.

A WEEK LATER Philip Weatherby sought his mother out in the living room of their flat. He blurted,

"Mamma I don't think I want to be married after all."

"What's that?"

"I don't think I want to be married Mamma."

"But how about Mary, Philip?"

"I don't know."

"You mean you haven't told her?"

"Not yet."

"Oh my dearest!" his mother cried. "And what are we to say to John?" Nevertheless there was something in her voice which could not be discouragement and when he replied it was in stronger if still bewildered tones.

"I thought you might have him round Mamma."

"Me?" she asked. "Tell him instead of you Philip?"

"Well of course it's for me to see Mary."

"But dear boy are you sure about all this?"

"I don't know."

"You don't know!" she echoed. "Oh my God where have things come to?"

"Mamma why is it Uncle Ned won't have anything to do with us?"

"Ned? You poor child he's simply an idiot and always was. How does he enter into this?"

"Not really."

"Oh my dearie," she announced, albeit almost gay "I feel

quite faint. Tell me though! Why must you turn round like you are doing?"

"I'm an awful nuisance I suppose?"

"Nuisance?" she exclaimed. "I hope I shall be the last to say that ever, your very own mother! No it's the shock."

"Somehow I didn't imagine you'd be altogether surprised."

"What was I to think?" she demanded. "Getting to your feet as you did in the middle of my party to my friends. I backed you up you must admit and I should hope so too, who would if I couldn't!"

"Oh you've been wonderful" he said with conviction. "You always are."

"I love you when you're like you're being" she said with fervour.

"Well, there's no closer family relationship after all."

"Yes but when you get to my age, have my experiences, though heaven forbid you should, my dear you'll realise I really do believe, that you only truly meet people even your nearest and dearest once or twice in a long long while and this is one of those minutes. I just never could feel you were suited to Mary."

"I don't think myself I'm right for her."

"Philip there's not a soul else is there? It can't be Bethesda?"

"Don't be so absurd Mamma."

"Forgive that" she said "I must be wandering. Oh I know Mary's a sweet child. But no one will stop me saying marriages between the children of old friends are so often a quite disastrous muddle."

"I hadn't worried about that side of it" he protested.

"Very likely not" she agreed. "All the same I did."

"In what way?"

"In no way at all Philip" his mother told him sharply. "Call it knowledge of the wicked world, call everything what you will, instinct might be the best name, but something whispered to me this would be wrong."

"You really have all along?"

"Oh I never interfere" she cried. "You can't say I've once come between you and something you've really wished. My dearest hope darling is to see you happy. Of course Mary's young. She'll soon get over things when the disappointment's gone. But what will John say?"

"Does this make it awkward for you?"

"I wouldn't say so quite" she replied. "I've known him now a great number of years. Still everything has to be done in a civilised way, I hope you realise Philip. Have you spoken to anyone yet?"

"Not a soul."

"That's so much gained then" she said. She paused, got a mirror out of her handbag and began to remake her face. Those great eyes were limpid with what seemed to be innocence.

"I mustn't be rushed" she announced at last.

"I know Mamma. I only came for advice."

"A little late for that?" she said tartly. "Now are you certain sure you've made up your own mind?"

"Well I'm not."

"Philip how can you say so when the girl's very sweet I know but a simpleton without a penny and not even really pretty."

Mr Weatherby became very dignified.

"Say what you like" he protested in sulky tones "I shall respect her all my life whatever happens."

"Which means that for two twos you'd wed her now?"

"I didn't say did I?"

"All right my dear" she said. "But you seem very touchy about this. She's a nice girl I agree yet I also know she's not nearly good enough for you. What are we to do about it, that is the question?"

"To be or not to be Mamma."

"Philip don't dramatise yourself for heaven's sake. This is no time for Richard II. You just can't go into marriage in such a frame of mind. Let me simply think!"

"What did you feel when you were getting married?"

"Is none of your damned business! Now leave me be, please my dear. I've got to use what wits I have left."

There was a silence while she covered her eyes with fat ringed fingers and he watched like a small boy.

"I shall have to ask John here to a meal" she decided at last.

"I don't somehow feel I could face him Mamma."

"Alone with me" she explained still from behind her hands. "Oh dear" she moaned "it's horribly like."

"What is?" he asked.

"Something years ago" she answered.

At this moment the door opened without a sound and her daughter crept through, a forefinger to the lips, obviously in the middle of a game.

"Hi-ya Pen" Mr Weatherby gravely said.

Mrs Weatherby screamed. Her hands went to her ears. "You sweet darling" she cried "what time is it? You mustn't come down now! So important. Philip and I are talking."

The child considered them out of her enormous eyes. Then she as softly withdrew still signalling silence.

"Mummy'll come up and read to you when you're in bed" the mother called after her. "God forgive me" she said in a lower voice "the little saint coming down like that has driven every idea right out of my poor mind."

"But Mamma you can't truthfully blame Mary for having no money of her own. Who is there has these days?"

"What's that got to do with it?" she asked from the midst of an obvious abstraction.

"Just a moment ago you said against Mary she didn't have a penny to her name."

"Philip" she cried "don't clutter me up with detail. Besides I always imagined you must keep some rags and tatters of family feeling left, of keeping up the name. No you'll please let me think."

He bit his nails.

"John has his awkward moments you know" Jane murmured at last.

"Always seemed fairly straightforward when I've seen the man" her son wearily protested.

"Which is all you know about people Philip. Oh dear for the matter of that what do we all of us know about anyone?"

"Well Mamma you're able to read me like the palm of your own hand."

"I'm not sure I can now Philip."

There was another pause.

"Then do you truly think I should go to a fortune teller?" his mother asked.

"If you feel it might help" the son replied.

"They sometimes give such bad advice and it's cruel hard to go against what they've said" she muttered. She removed the hand she held to her forehead, shading her eyes. He anxiously examined her face. But it could not be said there was any change in the expression. Sweetness and light still reigned supreme with perhaps a trace of mischief at the corners of a generous mouth.

"You'll have to tell Mary first" Mrs Weatherby announced. "Then and only then can I ask John to dinner. But what if he won't come?"

"Oh I know I shall have to see him Mamma!"

"You're to do nothing of the kind dearest until I've got my little oar in. I'll manage John I should hope after all these years, or I very much hope so. No I shall have to be ill. Not that I won't be really ill by that time, sick to death in my poor mind."

"I'm dreadfully sorry."

"Nonsense" she cried gaily. "Come over to me" she ordered. When he sheepishly rose she kissed him on his forehead then made him sit by her side. "What am I here for after all? Oh dear but isn't it going to be rather exciting and dreadful!"

Then she must have had a return to an earlier fear.

"My poor boy you're sure you haven't interfered with

128

the girl in any way?" she asked with averted head, laying a hand on his arm.

"Interfered? What d'you mean? She was the keenest on the whole idea as a matter of fact."

"Knowing you oh so well as I do I'm almost certain you've misunderstood me Philip. No I meant you haven't made love to her in that way have you?"

"Me? God no. It wouldn't have been right."

"I thought so" and she sighed. She turned her eyes back on him with a sorrowing look. "Yes" she said "you make some of it ever so much easier. I wonder if any of this would have happened if I'd married again and there'd been a man about the house."

"What difference could he have made? It's my life surely?"

"For you to live if you want to live" she answered.

"Of course I wish to. I'm not ill am I?"

"Now dearest you're not to turn sour and desperate just because you've got yourself into rather a silly little mess and have to come to me to get you out of things. How would everything have looked if we'd had it announced in the Press, tell me that?"

"Oh don't!"

"Quite Philip dear and I think you've been very wise, almost clever when all's said and done. But you've not breathed a word even to Liz are you sure?"

"Me? Why should I?"

"Or Maud Winder's girl? What's her name?"

"Certainly not."

"That's something certainly then!"

"You know I always tell you first Mamma."

"Bless you and so you should."

"But how does Miss Jennings come into this?"

"Dearest you'd never understand" she said. "Not in your present mood."

"Oh if you want to make mysteries" he objected.

"Now Philip I simply won't have it" she protested in a

bright voice. "You get yourself into a desperate tangle without a single word to me, you come out with things in public as though you were the only one concerned and at last you come to your mother and who wouldn't, oh I don't blame you there, to extricate yourself from whatever it may be; then you ask what's what, who's who and details of everything passing through my poor head, – have some consideration dearest for the poor person you're speaking to" she said happily "or I'm very much afraid you won't be able to do much with your life."

"Sorry" he muttered.

"After all I shan't be here forever" she added with a quick shadow of distaste passing across her lovely features.

"Don't" he groaned.

She patted the arm she had been holding.

"You mustn't take all this too seriously Philip" she comforted. "Not since you've promised me no actual harm's been done."

"But I've been so worried over little Pen" he wailed.

"God bless the little soul" Mrs Weatherby replied. "What about her, the saint?"

"When she was dead keen on being bridesmaid!"

"Bridesmaid? Who to?"

"Why Mary and me of course. You know how Penelope was!"

"Now really Philip" his mother protested and showed the first true signs of impatience she had displayed, "if I can't manage my own daughter who can, what use am I? We'll soon snap her out of that" she said stoutly. "You'll see if we don't."

THE NEXT SUNDAY John Pomfret and Miss Jennings were seated at their usual table. There was as yet no sign of Jane Weatherby or Mr Abbot. Thick fog curtained from without the windows that looked over the Park.

"But my dear" Liz was saying "what d'you propose?"

"In which way?" he asked.

"I mean how are you going to live?"

"Just the same as ever I imagine. We're all slaves to this endless work work work nowadays aren't we?"

"Then who will look after you?"

"Oh I expect I shall get by Liz. After all at my age it's the children's happiness is the thing."

"What nonsense you do talk John! It's even disgraceful from a man who's in the prime of life, and the more so when as I believe you realise yourself there's not a word of truth in all this you're saying."

He laughed. "Well" he reasoned "the children have to marry some time haven't they, sooner rather than never – I mean later" he corrected himself and gave Miss Jennings a short cool stare which she returned. "And when they do or while they're doing it we have to take a back seat with the best grace in the world."

"I don't think Jane is, John."

"Now you know how fond old Jane still keeps of the limelight."

"That's hardly what I meant dear. No she's telling almost everyone she'll stop this marriage by any means fair or foul."

He laughed louder. "Now darling whoever even suggested that?"

"It's all over London John."

"Be damned for a yarn" he said and a certain grimness underscored his voice. "I've seen this happen before. When the tongues start clacking then's the time for all good men and true to look to their powder and see it's dry."

"And make sure it isn't blank shooting or whatever that's called" Miss Jennings sweetly said.

He frowned. "Which sounds ominous. Did Jane speak to you Liz?"

"Oh no I'd be the last person, surely you realise dear! But she did get hold of that beastly Maud Winder which is why I was so careful just now to say Jane was telling almost everyone."

"But the whole thing is totally absurd Liz darling. I only had dinner with Jane last Tuesday and we discussed arrangements for literally hours on end."

"Did you go into detail?"

"Well no not exactly."

"Then there you are you see!"

"But you can't rush these matters Liz. There's every sort and kind of point to settle. And after all the children have really got to think their own problems out for themselves. Our or rather my function is to assist where I can, God help me."

"What did Jane actually say John?"

"Oh I don't know. She may be a bit confused of course, which is only natural but I know my Jane, she's fundamentally sound. Nothing wrong with her here" he said tapping the waistcoat pocket over his heart.

Miss Jennings made a noise between a groan and a snort. He did not seem to listen.

"I'd never mention it darling" he went on "but as I expect you've already heard, Jane and I had quite an affair once years ago and I think I know her as well as any man ever does know a woman."

"Which is why I asked what you meant to do with yourself."

"How d'you mean Liz?"

"Well I've realised all along you wouldn't put up with Jane's plotting so I was sure the marriage would go through you see."

"Thanks again," he said in a dry tone of voice.

"And now I want to know how you propose to manage?"

"Thanks again" he repeated.

"Now John don't be beastly" she protested. "Surely I've the right, or haven't I? Who is going to look after you?"

"When all's said and done Mary never did the cooking Liz."

"Oh I realise if anything happens to one of your poor faithful women like happiness or marriage or both, if that should conceivably be possible, then you can go and eat in your club where you'll get better food than ever we can provide you with, but who's to send your suits to the cleaners?"

"They have a weekly service."

She laughed. "No John you're not to be loutish" she cried. "You know exactly what I'm driving at."

"Who's to put out my slippers in front of the fire you mean?"

"Well yes if you like."

"My dear no one's ever done that for me in my life and it's too late now."

"Which just shows you simply won't have comfort even at the smallest price" she said. "You are all the same. You'd rather be miserable alone in a hovel of a room than put up with having a woman about to make it home."

"How little you know" he replied and gave what was obviously a mock sigh.

"But you'll find yourself terribly lonely, you know you will."

"Be nothing new in that" he said with a sort of bravado.

"You'd rather stay by your own on a desert island than give in to Jane wouldn't you? Now tell me."

"I suppose they must have been held up in the fog" he replied looking for Richard Abbot and Mrs Weatherby.

"Heaven pity me" she sighed. "Oh but you can be maddening sometimes!"

He leant forward, put a hand over hers.

"I'm so sorry darling, you see it's not my life, I haven't the right but Jane and I went slap through things when I last saw her and of course she's simply delighted with Mary. Strictly between you and me she's been worried about Philip and as a matter of fact I didn't much care for the boy myself at one period if you remember. Marriage'll be just the thing for him."

There was something in his speech which did not carry conviction, nevertheless Miss Jennings said "Go on, do. This is a distinct improvement."

He laughed. "Don't all you women get excited over weddings!"

"Well of course. What else d'you expect? Now go on."

"There's not a syllable more to tell just this minute. The second I have anything like a date or the name of the church, even where they propose to live I'll pass it on at once. But you know how jealous Jane can be, how particularly cagey where her own or her children's affairs are concerned. Why some days I myself hardly dare ask how little Penelope happens to feel. No, the less said at the moment the better."

"Then what about Maud Winder?"

"Oh this will cook her goose with Jane right enough. You just wait till she hears."

"But you promise if things won't run smoothly you shan't let Jane ride rough shod over all your plans."

"My darling Liz I've known her for literally ages. I might even understand Jane better than you."

"Don't keep on John throwing that beastly old affair of yours with the woman plumb in my face. I really rather wish you wouldn't!"

136

"OK I won't."

"Because heaven knows I'm no prude but there are parts of that story which aren't even, darling, for my tender ears."

He laughed. "I'm so sorry" he said.

"Well you'd better be" she answered and looked as though she sulked. There was a pause while he drummed on the table with his fingers.

"And have you got a list out, of the presents sweet Mary will want?" she asked.

"Not yet as a matter of fact."

"Blankets bathtowels and so forth? It makes such a difference because otherwise in spite of two wars she may get nothing but glass."

"I'll remember" he promised.

A FEW DAYS LATER Mrs Weatherby had John Pomfret to dinner alone for the third time after Philip had announced the engagement.

"Well Jane" he asked "have they said anything to you? Because I'm still without news at all."

"My poor heart goes out to them" she murmured.

"They seem to be taking their time certainly. But as you said the other day perhaps that's no bad thing in itself."

"It's not the two of them I worry over my dear so much as yourself." Her manner was unusually restrained, serious even.

He laughed uneasily. "How's this?" he cried.

"What on earth's to become of you when your girl goes?"

"But Jane Mary's not my cook."

"No John you're not to make a joke about it" she said although there was little mirthful in his attitude. "You owe your own self the sacred duty of seeing to yourself" she argued with a sweet sincerity. "I know children must marry some day bless them, but we do have the right to ask what is to become of our own lives."

"Yet not the right to ask that question of them Jane."

"My dear you are so much cleverer that you must bear with me. I never suggested anything of the kind I'm sure, now did I? I simply want to be told what you propose to do with yourself, that's all."

"Carry on as usual I suppose."

"Changing maids every eight weeks John?"

"Oh don't!" he cried. "No I had the idea I might drift along to the Club perhaps for a bit."

"And what sort of life is that for a man?" she demanded. "Besides you know you can't afford standing drinks to all and sundry every hour of the day and night."

"They have their licensing laws too you know."

"Stuff and nonsense! Don't tell me those men pay the smallest attention to stupid little regulations. No it would be so bad for you John."

"Then how d'you propose I should live?"

"I've simply no idea darling which is why I'm so terribly worried."

"Well I'm most flattered. Everyone seems to want to be told how I can manage. I just hadn't considered it, that's all."

"And you'll have had offers of help no doubt?"

"My dear if ever you hear of a responsible woman, what we used to call a cook general in the old days, who'll have nothing whatever to do in the daytime on vast wages, then you'll be my saviour."

"That wasn't what I meant in the least."

"But Jane I can't run to the expense of a married couple."

"And have the husband drinking your gin and rowing with his wife all day, I should think not indeed!"

"What did you have in mind then?"

"Marriage John."

"There can't be a double ceremony, they're so vulgar. Besides who'd have me?"

"Are you going to marry your Liz my dear?"

"Now Jane what is all this?"

"You should grant me certain privileges my loved one" she said staring at him until he looked away. "The years as they roll on give me a sort of wretched right" she announced. "And I'll not sit idly by and see you make yourself miserable just because Mary says she must leave home."

"There's no question, none at all!"

"But yes! Oh my dear you're going to be so lonely!"

"About Liz I mean."

"Are you sure?"

"No Jane how can you say am I sure? I still know what goes on around me I should hope."

"Does one ever?"

"I swear to you not a word's been said."

"Now John that makes not a scrap of difference, does it?"

"Yet to get married you have to say so don't you?"

"It's the final thing you say, yes."

"You will go on talking in riddles Jane."

"My dear I give you simple plain common or garden sense. You are like all men, lawyers every single one. You think there's no contract until you've said yes or had your answer but the chances are you've unofficially sworn yourself away for ever all unbeknownst quite months before. Which makes it so wicked when men try and back out."

"Now Jane to what is this referring?"

"Nothing my dear, at all."

"You were."

"On my honour. The past's past. The little I'm saying is she has her heart set on you."

"Well I suppose I might do worse at that."

"There you go, utterly sweet, completely deceitful!"

He laughed. "But you just put the idea right into my mind" he objected.

"I did nothing of the sort. And John don't bridle in that delighted way when I suggest someone might like to be married to you. I can't bear false modesty, which can be one of your little faults my dear. There are literally thousands of unattached women sitting by their telephones this very minute waiting for the call that never comes."

"I wish I met 'em."

"Don't be so tiresome please" she said. "Who d'you think you are anyway?"

"Well who then?"

"A most attractive man whose family life may just be about to be broken up from all accounts."

"You flatter me."

"No John you simply shall not take this stupid silly line. To all sorts and kinds of horrors waiting in their lairs you're a whole line of goods freshly come into the swim."

"Oh now you must grant me some powers of choice."

"But that's exactly it, I don't. How can I? You're only making fun while they're in wait there with the dread wretched lives they lead – no to give the present government its due they always did though it's not for me to praise politicians God help us, – those frightful endless days and nights have taught them so they're on watch for the slightest sign of backsliding."

"Now Jane you really can't make poor Liz out into a harpy or a pike!"

"Can't I!"

"You may not like her, she might not be the sort of person for you but at least she's not that kind."

"Well my dear" she agreed "you know how I always do go rather far. Mr Thicknesse has often told me. 'Dear lady' he's said and isn't it fantastic there are still people to call one that, 'your tongue will one day cost a deal of money'. It never has yet you know but then perhaps one's friends are more loyal than sometimes we suppose. You see I expect they must be. Because when I say what I do about Liz I don't really mean anything, only that she's such a horrid beast who simply oughtn't to be alive."

"No Jane there are occasions you can go too far!"

There was a pause which she filled by getting him more sherry.

"I'm sorry John but I mean every word for the best."

"Doesn't one always? Is that a valid excuse?"

"She doesn't."

"Then what exactly do you hold against the poor woman?"

"She's not poor, she's even very attractive in her own way, though of course she must have been to have the success she has. Oh what it takes to keep on learning one isn't the only pebble on the beach!"

"You don't suppose Dick Abbot is enamoured?" he asked with a degree of sarcasm in his voice.

"Richard?" she cried. For a moment she returned to her usually gay manner. "That sweet man! Never in the whole wide world!! How could he be?"

"Then Jane you just can't really accept any soul who sees Liz?"

"What d'you mean? That I care who she sees?"

"No quite" he agreed in a small voice.

"All I said was" she went on "and presuming oh yes I am on old friendship was that she couldn't, mustn't be the one for you, – I think I mean mustn't, really John darling!"

"And why? How mustn't?"

"But the woman drinks."

"Now Jane that's most unfair. You know she never has."

"I'm very sorry to say I know nothing of the kind."

"Good God then where and when?"

"My dear John! In the bedroom I expect."

"How can you speak of her bedroom?"

"Why should I know? I don't get in it."

"No Jane this is honestly almost unpleasant. We might, we may from time to time have had something for each other, Liz and I, but really I don't feel you have the right . . ."

"Don't I darling?"

"In what way then?"

"If I see you take a wrong turn, after all these years can't I say what I feel?"

"But we're here tonight to talk about the children."

"And isn't that just what we are discussing John?"

"No we never seem to get away from my own marriage which I give you my word is the first I've heard and which seems to be Liz all the time."

"Do you maintain she doesn't drink then John?"

"Well she certainly wasn't bottled at Eddie's as Maud Winder said she might be."

"How can you tell?"

"But I was there Jane."

"I'm going to say something darling may make you rather cross. It's simply that when you're out with her you sometimes are inclined to take a drop too much yourself."

"Oh now Jane this is preposterous! I wasn't that way at Eddie's."

"How can you possibly judge my dear? Oh I'm not trying to make out you are a soak like poor William Smith, so much so that his wife had to leave him, you remember sad Myra – what's happened to her – couldn't face pouring the whisky down his throat when he lost his arms? I'm not pretending anything. I only maintain which I shall until the day I die that when you're out with the woman, and it's not necessarily anything noticeable, you aren't sometimes a very good judge perhaps of how much someone else has taken."

He swallowed air three or four times.

"I still don't see how all this has to do with Philip and Mary" he objected.

"I do" she said.

"Well how then?" he almost shouted.

"Now you're simply not to bully me in my own house"

she announced in a small voice. "I have such a headache into the bargain."

"I'm sorry Jane" he said, quieter.

There was a pause. After which she said in low tones, "I had no call to tell you what I did either."

"Oh I know you meant it for the best" he smiled.

"I not only meant it, it was best" she rejoined.

"Very well" he agreed. "But you might admit you could be wrong about Liz."

"Of course I may. Yet I'm not."

He swallowed air again. "All right darling" he admitted.

"That's better" she said.

"Still I don't get drunk Jane."

"No there I admit I went too far dear John. I got upset!"

"Dear me!" he smiled. "What we all go through when the children want to settle their lives for themselves."

"What we go through to avoid what we might have to go through" she took him up at once.

"Yes very well Jane" he agreed.

"Oh my headache is so bad" she said visibly wilting.

"You ought to lie down."

At this moment Isabella flung the door open to announce something in a flood of words, presumably that dinner was served. Mrs Weatherby thanked her.

"It's hammering round my head" she wailed.

"Why don't you go along then Jane?"

"D'you know I simply feel I must. But whatever will you think of me?"

"I'll bring you yours in on a tray."

"You'll do nothing of the kind" she objected. "What would Isabella simply think? No when I get one of my sick headaches I just can't eat anything. I must shut my poor aching eyes in the dark. But what will you do John dear? Oh how rude I am!"

"I can get a bite at the Club."

"Certainly not. No you'll dine here I insist. Not that it'll be worth having. Oh dear!"

"I'm so sorry Jane and I hope you'll be better tomorrow. Sure there isn't anything I've foolishly said?"

"How could there be? No you'll simply have to forgive."

While he kissed her cheek as she prepared to leave he ventured once more,

"And you've heard nothing fresh from the children?"

"Not a word" she replied, then disappeared tragically smiling.

SOON AFTER THIS, with the day's work done, Mary Pomfret came to her father when he was alone over an evening paper.

"Daddy is there any news?" she asked.

"Of the wedding stakes?" he cried. "But I have none."

"Because oh dear it's not going well I think Daddy!"

"Engagements never do my dear."

"You are such a comfort" she said. "And it's so complicated. Still I suppose everything always is."

"I nearly went mad when I became engaged to your mother."

"Did you? Oh Daddy what I want to know is the line Mrs Weatherby's taking?"

"Funny you should ask. I took old Dick Abbot out and put him that very question. I should think he sees more of Jane than anyone these days. He rather seemed to be of the opinion she hadn't quite made her mind up yet. Now you know I consider I can read Jane as well as the next man and I'd say myself she was enthusiastic, hand on my heart I would."

"Then you haven't heard this extraordinary story that Philip and I are really half brother and sister?"

"What?" he yelled and nearly shot out of his chair, crushing the newspaper in the process.

"Here let me do that" his daughter said and picked those sheets up to pat them flat again. She kept her eyes from off his face.

"If you would only tell me who'd said it then I'd have the law on 'em" he panted.

"My future mother-in-law" she murmured.

"Jane did! You can't be serious Mary!"

"Daddy, do say it isn't true!"

"True! You must be insane. Good God! Good God!!"

"Well is it?"

"No of course not."

"How can you be sure Daddy?"

"Because I am."

"I'm terribly sorry but you see this means rather a lot to me."

He controlled himself. "Of course, must do monkey" he said.

"And you couldn't possibly be?" she insisted.

"Oh well you know how things are" he lamely explained. "Jane and I certainly saw quite a bit of each other about that time, the time he was born I mean. But the thing's utterly preposterous."

"Because if it was true I don't think I could ever speak to you again."

"I do realise that Mary. Look you've got to listen to me. I know you'll think I have a special reason for telling you this but you must believe your father!"

At this point she handed the newspaper back neatly folded.

"Oh thanks" he said. It seemed as if his train of thought had been broken for when he went on he said,

"Jane surely never told you?"

"No she didn't. I went down to ask her at Brighton as a matter of fact and when I got there I simply found I hadn't the gumption."

"I'm not surprised Mary." He tried a laugh. She actually giggled a moment but still kept her eyes from his. "I must say!" he added and laughed louder. She did not respond however and he returned to his serious manner.

"Who's been hinting?" he demanded.

"Well as a matter of fact Philip mentioned something."

"Philip" he echoed in noticeably brighter tones. "How can he know at his age?"

"No Daddy you're not to laugh! You remember what I told you, I'd never speak to you again."

"I'm not laughing" he defended himself. "But you'll agree my dear it isn't a very pleasant thing to be confronted on without a word of warning."

"And not nice for me either under the circumstances?"

"Frightful" he agreed. "My God I've never heard anything like it! But where did your Philip get this extraordinary notion?"

"From his mother I fancy."

"So that's how it originated! She didn't tell you then?"

"Oh no I've just said haven't I? I went down to see her in the hotel and then couldn't screw up my miserable courage."

"You're not to blame monkey good Lord! I should say not! But d'you mean to tell me Jane actually put it in so many words?"

"I'm not sure."

"Then darling you must make doubly certain."

"Why should I when you told me not a moment ago it could be."

"Could be what?"

"True Daddy."

"But my love I never said a word of the kind!"

"You did."

"How did I?"

"Just now when you admitted you'd seen a lot of her about that time."

"But the idea's perfectly ridiculous" he replied in blustering accents. "Why doesn't he come and ask me himself? I'd soon tell him."

"For the same reason I expect I couldn't bring myself with his mother. But oh Daddy do say all this isn't true."

"I've already told you. It's utterly ridiculous! I've never in my whole life heard such awful nonsense!"

"Then why did you say what you did?"

"Earlier on? For the simple reason this was the first time such an insane idea had ever been put to me. I was flabbergasted, absolutely stunned! And I'm so accustomed to the worst that for a second I even considered whether it mightn't be a fact. But I tell you what. You know about that time things were pretty strained between the four of us, I mean he wasn't even born then and his father began throwing writs about and cross-petitions, – we won't go into all the business now, what's over's over, enough's enough, – but if there could be a word of truth in this tale don't you agree Weatherby would have used your story? And he didn't! If you don't believe me go and ask Mr Thicknesse."

"Oh Daddy so you really don't think there's anything?"

"Of course not my dear. Lord but you had me thoroughly rattled for a minute."

"I'm such a nuisance" she wailed, gazing straight at him, her eyes full of tears.

"You aren't" he said. "Besides why don't you ask the others?"

"I have."

He looked at her very hard.

"And what did they say?"

"I went to Arthur Morris and Philip did too, separately of course. He told us both the same or so Philip swears."

"There you are then! With the poor fellow dying he'd surely never dare tell a lie."

"But Daddy how simply dreadful! He isn't is he?"

"So Liz says."

"He simply can't. He's so sweet!"

"That's the way things are my dear I'm afraid. Well we've all got to come to it. When he didn't turn up at Jane's party I thought he must be pretty bad. What's the ring you're wearing?"

"It's mine. I mean the engagement ring."

"Oh I say" he cried "and you never told. Here let's have a good look."

They bent their heads together over her left hand.

"Well well" he said. "This is quite pretty isn't it? How much did he pay?"

"That's my secret Daddy. We talked everything over of course. We decided we'd be insane to spend a lot of cash on what is out of date tripe. I never meant it to be more than just something to go on that especial finger."

"One bit of jewelry I always did swear could be worth a bust was the engagement ring."

"Oh I know you don't like it or him" she wailed, sharply withdrawing her hand.

"Now my dear" he interrupted "we can't have this! You're overwrought. Good God you've your own lives to lead haven't you? I think the good ring very suitable, so there."

"Do you" she murmured seeming mollified. "And you won't so much as breathe to Mrs Weatherby about the other business?"

"See here what sort and kind of a parent d'you take me for? Why naturally not" he replied.

KNOWING HIS DAUGHTER was to be out of London the next forty-eight hours on some trip in connection with her Government job Mr Pomfret at once got on the telephone to Jane and asked the lady round the next day to what he called a scratch meal at his flat.

After giving her a drink he led the way into the next room where a spectacular supper was laid out and which began with caviar. Once she had exclaimed at this and he had been able to sketch in the devious methods he employed to lay hands on such a delicacy, he so to speak cut right down into the heart of things by saying,

"Well I've seen the ring."

"Oh my dear" she replied "so have I!"

He considered Mrs Weatherby very carefully at this response but she was eating her sturgeon's eggs with a charming concentration that was also the height of graceful greed, her shining mouth and brilliant teeth snapping just precisely enough to show enthusiasm without haste, the great eyes reverently lowered on her plate.

"Did you help Philip choose?"

"Me? Dear no" she answered, carefully selecting a piece of toast. "I know better than to interfere ever" she said. "But you make me feel such a perfect fool John" she continued. "There was I the other evening wanted so much to be told how you would manage when you had to live alone and now you put me to absolute shame with a lovely choice meal like this."

"Oh we don't do it every day" he laughed then turned serious once more. "And do you like the ring Jane?"

"No" she said "who could? I was so vexed."

"I would only say it to you my dear" Mr Pomfret announced "but the boy must have gone to ———'s" and he gave the name of a shop which extensively advertised cheap engagement hoops.

She raised her eyes to his from the caviar with reluctance and a charming smile.

"One has to be so careful never to butt in" she explained "or rather, and am I being wicked, never to seem that one is arranging their little affairs for them. I tried to make him give dear Mary a solitaire darling Mother left me in her will

149

and that somehow I've not had the heart to sell." She now looked down at her plate again and went on unhurriedly eating caviar. Then she squeezed some more lemon with an entrancing grimace of alarm, presumably lest a drop lodge in the corner of an eye. "How delicious and good this is" she sighed.

"And Philip wouldn't have it?" he asked.

"Philip simply wouldn't" she confirmed.

There was a pause.

"Then I had so hoped" she calmly went on at last "for you know what he is about family feelings, – well I don't say this ring of Mother's was enormously valuable or of course it would have gone long before now, one can't go round London barefoot after all, – but in a way the thing's an heirloom and he'd only have had to get it lined because of course Mother had such small bones."

"You don't think Mary's fingers are like bananas?"

"John!" she screamed, eyeing him in alarm. "I don't find that funny do you!"

"Well all right then" he said. "But what are we to do about this ring he's given her?"

"Doesn't she like it?"

"You know how you felt just now yourself Jane."

"Oh yes but we mustn't make everything more difficult for them dear. You realise it's not going to be easy for those two sweet loves our being such old friends you and I. But has Mary actually put it into words about the thing?"

"No. How could she?"

"She's wonderful! So d'you think we would be absolutely wise to interfere?"

"Yet you can't let her walk round with that on her left hand Jane."

Mrs Weatherby faced him squarely at this.

"Wait a moment John please" she said in a level voice. "Exactly what have you on your mind?"

"Awkward" he grumbled. "Damned awkward! It's

simply as an old friend I feel that it may reflect on you and yours" he said.

She pushed away from in front of her the plate which by now was dry as if a cat had licked it.

"But my dear" she cried "on me? After all I've done? When he wouldn't have darling Mother's which I'm almost sure Mary has never even seen. You mean poor Philip's one's too cheap?"

"I do."

"I don't call fifteen guineas cheap."

"Not for what he got."

"Oh my dear I can't think when I've been so upset in my life" she gasped but not altogether convincingly.

He laid a hand over hers which she did not withdraw.

"To do a thing like that might come back on us both" he said.

"You mean our friends . . . ?"

"Yes."

"What does Liz say?" she asked.

"I don't know for the very simple reason that I haven't enquired" he answered. "And I shan't."

"So you're just guessing, is that it John?"

"I've lived long enough in our lot not to have to ask."

He proceeded to serve Mrs Weatherby with lobster mayonnaise.

"Well if it all doesn't come back on my poor shoulders . . ." she murmured. "When I've done nothing but my best."

"All the same Jane we must find something."

"But oh they're so independent" she wailed.

"Can't he give her another?"

"What with?"

"How d'you mean Jane, what with? You could sell the solitaire couldn't you and let him have the proceeds?"

"And he does go on so, that they must live on what they earn."

"Well my dear" he said "we haven't been into that

together yet have we? The last time you'd just come from seeing Thicknesse and didn't feel like it if you remember."

"No more I do now John."

"All right. I don't wish to press you. But we shall have to take some step about this engagement ring or we might be a laughing stock."

"John" she announced after a pause "sometimes I feel rather inclined to say 'damn the children, they're more trouble than they're worth'."

"Well I don't know about that Jane."

"Don't you? But why can't they do things the way we did?"

"Money I suppose. Besides I wouldn't care for 'em to get into the mess we got into."

"Now darling you're not to speak so of what is still absolutely sacred to me. How delicious this lobster is! Where did you go to find it?"

He told her.

She ate with evident appreciation.

"You don't care for Philip's hats either I hear?" she said sweetly.

"No more I do" Mr Pomfret replied.

"On the whole wouldn't you say John it's rather best for them to make their own mistakes?"

"It all depends."

"In what way dear?"

He turned very white.

"I don't want us to look ridiculous Jane!"

She raised her eyebrows and stared coolly at him.

"I'm not sure what you mean?" she said.

In a trembling voice, with an obvious and complete loss of temper he cried all at once,

"By trying to stop this marriage by saying as I'm told you are that Philip is my son."

She put knife and fork carefully down on the plate, turned her face half away from him, closed her eyes and waited in silence. Within twenty seconds two great tears had slipped from beneath black lashes and were on their way over her full cheeks, shortly followed by others. But she made no sound.

He blew his nose loudly, his colour began to come back. He watched. Soon his breathing became normal again.

"I'm sorry" he muttered at last.

"Excuse me" she said getting up from the table and hastened out of the room. He waited. He hung his head to listen, perhaps for the front door. When the bathroom lock clicked he appeared to relax.

Eventually she returned like a ship in full sail. He stood as she came in the door. She stopped close enough to hit him.

"How dare you!!" she hissed.

"Oh my dear I do apologise" he said and wrung his hands. "Last thing in the world I wished to blurt out."

"How dare you John!"

"Look here sit down once more Jane. That silly remark slipped from me I swear it!"

"I oughtn't to stay here another minute" she announced and sat in her place. He seated himself. He mopped at his face with a handkerchief. She watched her plate of lobster mayonnaise. "This is Liz's doing" she added.

"No Jane don't" he implored.

"Well that was her wasn't it?"

"Yes I suppose so."

She took up knife and fork again, began to push the food around the plate.

"I say it for your own good John" she said. "You should have nothing more to do with that young woman before she ruins you!"

"Now Jane" he cried raising a glass to his lips with trembling hands.

"Because when you allow the squalid girls you choose for your wicked selfish pleasures to interfere between my son and your girl then you aren't fit."

"And Richard Abbot?" he muttered.

"Is one of nature's gentlemen" she royally replied. "Now not another word of this or I leave at once never to step over your doorstep again."

After which the conversation limped for some time then she laughed and in another thirty minutes he tried a laugh and in the end as old friends they parted early without another mention of the children.

A WEEK LATER Miss Jennings did something she had never done before, she asked Richard Abbot round for a drink.

"Have you heard about poor darling John?" she said and giggled. "His doctor's told him he's got a touch of this awful diabetes."

"Good Lord, sorry to learn that."

She giggled again.

"No one knows. Of course he told me. I'm so very worried for him. Isn't it merciful they discovered about insulin in time?"

"No danger in diabetes nowadays" Mr Abbot agreed. "Rotten thing to catch though."

"How ought he to look after himself Richard?"

"Just take it easy and they can give themselves the injections."

"Themselves? Injections! Oh no surely a woman must do for them. I mean you can't jab a needle into your own arm surely?"

"Or a leg. That's what they say Liz."

"Of course there's Mary" Miss Jennings continued. "She could be the one until she actually marries Philip. But once those two get away on their own how will John manage Richard?"

"They can do it for themselves" he repeated.

"Does Jane know?"

"The way to give hypodermics? Couldn't say I'm sure."

"No no I naturally didn't mean was Jane a nurse. Has she heard d'you think?"

"Couldn't be certain. Not mentioned a word to me."

"Because I'll tell you what. John's having diabetes like this alters everything. There is bound to be a change in Jane's whole attitude to the children's marriage."

"Can't follow you at all."

"Oh but of course you do. Don't play the innocent Richard. She's been simply fixed on stopping it by every means. But now he'll need looking after, she won't leave Mary home to do the nursing."

"And d'you imagine John will have no say in that?" Mr Abbot enquired. "He's got you hasn't he? You'll have to take lessons Liz."

"He's got me all right" she said. "Yes. But have I got him, there's the question" and she laughed outright then at once grew serious once again.

"Then will he have terrible pricks all over his poor arms and legs?" she cried.

He gently laughed.

"Oh come Liz" he argued. "That's only a detail."

"A detail? Will there be something else as well?"

"No but what's the matter with a few dots on his skin?"

"I thought you meant he might have to have some other ghastly treatment Richard. I was so nervous for a minute. I believe you're teasing me you horrid man."

"You're all right Liz."

"I wish I was. Has Jane really said nothing to you about the marriage?"

"Not to me."

"Because she'll force it on now, you mark my words."

"Whatever she does is perfect by me Liz."

"Has there ever been anyone as loyal as you dear Richard! You are so good."

"Mind if I say something?"

"Of course not. How could I?"

"Might be you make too much of things."

"Oh come now Richard you aren't going to say 'mountains out of molehills', not as late in the day as this surely?"

"I could."

"But don't you see what's going on under your very own nose?" she goodhumouredly demanded.

"Cheer up" he said. "It needn't happen."

"And shan't if I have anything to do with things. I used to love old John. I can't bear to stand by and see him ruined."

Mr Abbot's eyes widened. He watched the woman with plain amazement and some cunning.

"Don't look at me as though you'd seen a ghost" Miss Jennings softly said. "I've been around all this time even if you have only just noticed."

"Sorry" he said at once. "But you're a surprising person Liz."

"Of course I am" she replied.

"You were keen enough on the children's marriage once" he pointed out.

"Well naturally" she answered.

"And now you want a girl of nineteen to stay at home single so as to give her father injections?"

"But John dines with Jane every other night already!"

"You and I couldn't stop them even if we wanted to."

"Perhaps not Richard" she admitted. "Still we might try and keep it at that and then they could conceivably quarrel over the arrangements even yet, who knows? Because I won't have those two children made into pawns, their whole lives I mean, their own futures, just for Jane to play sicknurse to poor John."

"I thought you were the one who was so keen on Philip marrying Mary."

"I was" she wailed.

"Well then why change when the wind seems to blow the other way? We aren't weathercocks after all."

"I am where John's concerned."

156

"But you just said Liz . . ."

"I know" she interrupted "but I simply can't bear the thought of that woman sticking needles in his arm."

"Liz!" he warned.

"Oh what must you think of me?" she cried. "Yet I just can't help myself and you know she'd give him blood-poisoning."

"If he won't learn to manage by himself why shouldn't you be the one for the chap?"

"Would you like that best Richard?"

He paused and looked about.

"Me?" he asked at last.

"Yes you."

"How do I come in?"

"Oh well if you won't talk" she replied with a small voice. "Of course I've no right to go on like this. Yes well there you are."

"Hope I didn't seem rude at all" he said at once. "Excuse me will you? Fact is I've got a feeling no one has any right to interfere with the lives of others."

"But don't they interfere all the time in yours?"

"Shouldn't be surprised."

"Well then!"

"There's no 'well then' about this" he protested sharply. "Can't be too grateful to old Jane" he muttered "and I like those two kids."

"Richard you are sweet and wonderful" she said with apparent sincerity shortly after which, and time was getting on, he went off alone to dine at the Club.

UPON WHICH Mrs Weatherby again asked John Pomfret to dinner.

"Oh my dear I'm so worried about little Penelope once more" she began as soon as he came in.

"Why how's that?" he asked.

"It's all to do with this horrid new thing you've got" Jane explained. "The poor sweet will insist on sticking pins into herself now."

He laughed rather bitterly.

"Oh dear" he said.

"I know it's dreadful of me" she admitted. "There you are chock full of diabetes so to speak yet I can't but worry my heart out over the little saint. What d'you suppose will stop her?"

"How d'you mean?"

"Well she can't just go on pretending to inject herself all of every day can she? It's even so dangerous. She might get blood-poisoning. And oh my dear in what way will you manage yourself? Have you thought of that? Because after a little while there won't be any free space left?"

He laughed once more.

"There is the diet treatment" he suggested.

"Then do tell Pen so with your own lips" she pleaded.

"But Jane you wouldn't want the child to starve herself?" Mrs Weatherby chuckled.

"Good Lord what a perfect fool I am not to have thought of that" she admitted. "If you hadn't said we might've had her really on our hands! Now darling how about you? Are you all right?"

"Well yes I imagine so" he conceded. "Of course it's a bore but one has to be thankful it's not worse I suppose."

"You're perfectly wonderful the way you take everything John" Mrs Weatherby insisted.

"But who told Penelope about me?" he asked.

"I did" the mother wailed. "You know how truly fond of you she is, why, she dotes on you John, and I wanted to make Pen a little bit sad – you see at that instant minute she was creating such a dreadful noise and racket, so I told her your news the little pet, and my dear it came off all too

158

well, she's been quiet as a mouse jabbing great pins in her leg ever since."

Mrs Weatherby gaily laughed and so did John Pomfret. Then she went on quite serious again,

"And if Pen let go, should one of those pins get inside her, it might even travel right to her little heart, darling isn't that too awful just for words?"

Jane turned her eyes, which immediate fright made still more enormous, full on him.

"Don't you worry" he said smiling.

"Yet darling mother had one in her all her life. It entered through the seat."

"She sat on a pin?" he interrupted, broadly smiling now.

"Yes she was one of the first to be X-rayed" Mrs Weatherby continued, "it travelled all over, just think, and then when she died she had pernicious anaemia after all, poor wonderful darling that she was."

"I expect Pen will be all right" he comforted.

"She'll have to be" Mrs Weatherby replied with great conviction. "John tell me about yourself. How serious is it really?"

"Well I have to take things easy for a bit you know. I can't throw up the office worse luck but I'll have to be careful in the evenings."

"It's extraordinary my dear your saying what you have just done about the office" Mrs Weatherby exclaimed. "I was only thinking the other day over your sweet Mary and how bad all this working life is for these girls."

"Why Jane what on earth do you mean?"

"Oh nothing, certainly nothing which concerns the ghastly talk we had last time about their plans or rather the endless lack of plans they seem to have. But John don't you think she should get right away before she settles down?"

He turned rather white.

"Rid ourselves of her for a bit?" he enquired.

"Now don't turn so damned suspicious" she said equably. "I wouldn't be in the least surprised if my little plot didn't bring precious Philip up to the boil though poor darling I don't really know how much else he can do when he's already proposed and given her a ring." At this Mr Pomfret seemed on the point of speech but Jane waved him down. "No" she gaily cried "I won't allow you, just let it pass, I was only joking. But you know what things are for a girl. And whatever we may do to help them, in the end there probably won't be much money. No I think she ought to have a change first."

"She's only just out of the nursery Jane where she's rested all her short life so far."

"Then they often start a baby so much too soon" Mrs Weatherby went on imperturbably, "terribly exhausting after all the excitement of the wedding. No John no you really don't understand about girls, how should you? And after that it's just one long grind darling until they're too old to enjoy a thing. I think you should send her to Italy for at least two months."

"But the money" he cried.

"Sell a pair of cufflinks" she sweetly suggested. "As a matter of fact I had a letter from Myra Smith only yesterday. She's been in Florence all this time, fancy that! She wants to hear of an English girl to stay with her and as a return she asks to be taken in herself over here, she wants to see London again she says."

"But good God I couldn't put Myra up at my place. It wouldn't look decent!"

"With Mary not there, married to Philip you mean? Oh well I'd negotiate my fences as they came if I were you John. Still, if it amounted to all that I could take the woman in here."

"I can't quite seem to see . . ." Mr Pomfret began when Jane interrupted him.

"I know you can't" she said "but you must remember you've been so fortunate all your life and now you have a touch of illness I simply shall not allow it to warp your judgement. Or Arthur Morris now? He has no use for his flat while he's at the clinic. He could lend it to Myra."

"My dear Jane we've to get Mary out in Italy for two months first surely. In any case I'm sorry to say there's bad news about poor old Arthur. He's not so well at all they tell me."

"No no John" she cried "I simply don't want to hear!"

"Yes" Mr Pomfret went on "it seems they've told him he'll have to have his leg off now above the knee."

She covered her ears with two fat white hands.

"Too too disagreeable" she moaned. "And now that all one's friends have reached middle age is there to be nothing but illness from now on, first Arthur then my dear you? Oh tell me are you really all right?"

He laughed. "There's nothing the matter with me compared with poor old Arthur" he assured Mrs Weatherby.

"That's all right then" she replied lowering her hands. "Let me get you another drink." When she had brought this and placed it on the table by his chair she leant down and put her cheek against his own. Not for many years had she done the same. He closed his eyes. Her skin was the texture of a large soft flower in sun, dry but with the pores open, brilliant, unaccountable and proud.

"You swear you're all right?" she murmured.

"Oh yes."

"Because you of all men just must be" she said, gently withdrawing. For the rest of the time she did not mention Liz or the children and was particularly attentive.

A FEW EVENINGS LATER Mr Pomfret said to his girl Mary,

"Monkey I've been thinking things over and I should like you to go to Italy for a bit."

"Italy Daddy? Whatever for?"

"Oh nothing in particular. I thought it might be a good idea that's all."

"But why?"

"Wouldn't you care to travel then?"

"Daddy, did Mrs Weatherby also think of this?"

"Good Lord no Mary. Whoever put it in your head?"

"I just wondered that's all" she explained rather grimly.

"Myra Smith would have you at her place in Florence" Mr Pomfret went on "and you could do the picture galleries and things."

"Be serious Daddy. However could I get leave from my job?"

"I've thought of that too" her father replied. "Why don't you simply throw it up? You slave frightfully hard all day at menial tasks; there's no future there Mary as you yourself said the other day."

"Give up my work!" she gasped.

"But they pay you so badly. When you're married you may have to find something that brings in more."

"I'm glad someone has mentioned the marriage at last" she said. "Just recently there's been almost what I'd call a plot of silence about it."

"I was only talking to Jane on the subject the other night dearie."

"When she suggested I should go?"

"Now monkey I've already told you. It was my plan and she thoroughly agreed as a matter of fact. Indeed it was herself said there could be no manner of fun in getting married these days, I mean things aren't easy still, girls have an awful grind to put a home together. Take a few weeks off before you settle down."

"But could you afford it?"

"Oh we'll find ways and means I suppose."

"Wouldn't it be better though to save for the honeymoon if you're so keen for me to go to Florence?"

This silenced him a moment.

"No" he replied eventually. "Venice for newly marrieds, Florence for girls before they become engaged. Next time you go round to see Philip just ask their Isabella!"

"I'm not sure I want to go Daddy."

"Oh go on and have some fun."

"I don't wish for fun, or rather that kind of gay time. I'm not sure it would be enjoyable."

"But you haven't ever been abroad dear, you've not seen anything in your life. As things are you may never have the chance again."

"What made you get this idea Daddy?"

"Nothing. I just had it" he said in rather a surly voice.

"You didn't speak to Philip about Italy?"

"I promise not."

"Because he mightn't like my throwing up the job. He's funny that way you know."

"But if he heard you were to go to a better paid one?"

"My dear you don't understand at all. He's very serious minded Daddy. He thinks we ought all to be in Government jobs."

"What's so odd about that? Practically everyone is."

"Well I'm not going to try and explain Philip to you! Who is this Mrs Smith anyway? Would she like me?"

"Oh we all knew her at one time. Can't say I saw much of Myra ever. She was more a friend of Jane's to tell the truth."

"There Mrs Weatherby comes into it again" his daughter murmured.

Mr Pomfret seemed to ignore the comment.

"Rather a sad story" he mused aloud. "Drove poor William hopelessly to drink then left him when the poor fellow was done for. She's quite different now of course from all I hear, settled down quite remarkably from many accounts. You ought to ask old Arthur Morris. He keeps in touch I believe."

"But has she a flat or what?"

"My, aren't you being practical all of a sudden love! I suppose it's this wedding business."

"Now you of all people are not to laugh at me! I'm sure someone in this family must be sensible and it won't ever be you darling as you'll admit."

"All right poppet" he laughed. "So anyway you don't say no to your Italian trip."

"I haven't said yes have I?"

"I don't want you hanging about while there's still so much to be decided Mary" he declared and was serious. "Everything's going to come out the way you want, you'll see my dear but it might be best if you kept out of the picture a few weeks."

"Oh Daddy you do think so?"

"I do."

"I see. Well I'll try and get after Arthur Morris. When all's said and done I can't make up my mind without I know something about this Mrs Smith can I?"

At which Miss Pomfret retired to bed.

FOUR DAYS LATER Miss Jennings was giving Mr Abbot dinner at her flat.

"Yes there she went poor child" Liz wailed "right through the teeming rain to ask him and when she got to the clinic she walked straight into that lift large enough to take a hearse. Dear Mary rose all the way to his floor and you know the long passages they have there, well she wandered down and knocked on Arthur's door just as she had done so often."

"Were you with her?" Richard Abbot interrupted.

"No Mary told me. Who else has she got these days the darling? And when the child knocked a nurse happened to come from a next room and cried out 'oh but you can't go in now'. Anyway Mary was shown to one of those alcoves off the corridor with three armchairs and the occasional table. There she sat thinking Arthur was to be washed or something when at last the sister came. It makes one's heart sink Richard to picture it, the poor love thrown over by her own father, oh she has told me all, waiting to ask so much she shouldn't know of the one person who could give it as she thought, poor Arthur, then the nursing sister saying she was afraid Mary could go in no more!! When the child wanted to be told why, it all came out of course, he'd just died Richard, not an hour ago, wasn't it frightful!"

"Yes I heard at the Club. I'm very sorry" Mr Abbot said. "What was the cause?"

"Well the extraordinary part is they didn't have the address of a single one of his relatives, they wanted Mary at the clinic to give them names but he was absolutely alone Richard, if you'd been at the grave this afternoon with me you'd have seen there wasn't a soul except old friends, isn't that perfectly awful? Of course Jane cried enough for his mother and sister combined if they'd been spared, – oh I know what you're about to say" and she solemnly raised a trembling hand to restrain him "I expect she may have been quite genuine, minded Arthur being dead I mean, but naturally John had to make all the arrangements just as though he was the next of kin."

There was a pause while Liz got out a handkerchief which she pushed with a forefinger at the corner of her eye.

"So what did Arthur die of?" Mr Abbot enquired in a neutral voice.

"The clot. Flew straight to his heart" she replied tragically. "Oh Richard it makes one wonder who will be next?"

"These things happen" the man answered. "But what did Mary wish to know?"

"Well I suppose you'll think this is none of my business" she said. "At the same time, fond as I am of John and Jane, I'm not so blind Richard I can't see all that goes on right in front of my own nose. I don't care what you say my dear but Jane's sending the child away to Italy and making her throw up the job for it, must be clearing the decks for action like they do in the Navy."

"How can Jane send Mary?"

"But Richard by working on John. I never even see him now. The moment those two children tried to get engaged Jane has had the man living in her pocket."

"I know what you mean" Mr Abbot admitted at last, though he seemed to speak with reluctance. "No more than natural all the same."

Mr Abbot appeared ill at ease.

"Natural?" she cried. "Yes I suppose so in a farm yard sort of fashion."

"Then you think it's all come to life once again between them."

"If I said 'over my dead body' then I might be six foot underground this minute" she replied and they both laughed.

"Sounds bad" he muttered.

"Well every word's true isn't it Richard?"

"Shouldn't be surprised" he answered with a return to his usual manner. "As that film star said when he landed this side of the Atlantic and the reporters asked about the lady in his life, 'I'm just a thanks a million man'. Damn good you know."

"But are you all right Richard?"

"All right?"

"Yes, in your own health and strength? Here's John with diabetes and Arthur Morris gone. Who's next?"

He laughed. "Me? I'm fit as a fiddle" he protested.

She laughed. "Now don't you just be too sure" she warned. "Though one of the things I so like about you Richard is you keep your figure beautifully, still look really athletic I mean."

"Pure luck" he replied. "Some are born that way. Well then about Mary? What did she want of Arthur?"

"They're sending the child off to this sort of Mrs Smith

in Florence. I never knew the woman so Mary couldn't ask me though she has since. All I could tell the child was, Myra used to be a great friend of the whole bunch while I was still doing French grammar in my rompers. So you see Richard, Mary the poor angel doesn't know what's up. Frightfully wicked they are."

"Expect everything's for the best. After all Liz whoever can tell what may come?"

"Oh I agree more than you'll ever realise. Yet how wrong to play with one's own children's feelings!"

"They don't. They're thinking about themselves and I don't altogether blame 'em."

"I realise everyone does" she admitted. "I quite see even with a baby in arms a great deal of oneself comes into it. But they really ought not to work on Philip. They'll ruin his life, what there is left."

"D'you reckon John realises what he's up to?"

"Not consciously of course, yet he can't be so reckless he mayn't take advice. Oh Richard he's gone back so the last few months! Was it his diabetes d'you suppose?"

"Diabetes?"

"Weakened him my dear. I can't abide men who turn wet. He's come to be like a sponge, going round to her place every other day, sometimes twice in the twenty four hours as he does."

"Nothing we can do."

"There is then!"

"How's that Liz?"

"Just you wait and see Richard." She laughed light-heartedly.

"Well you've been wrong once and you can be again" he said.

"When?" she demanded.

"Not so long ago you told me since John had diabetes Jane would hurry the marriage along between Mary and Philip for reasons of her own."

"I also said she'd been against it Richard."

167

"All right" he agreed. "On the other hand you tell me now Jane is packing Mary off to her father's old battlefields so that she can marry John."

"Because I've begun to see Jane must have it both ways. She'll prevent the wedding so that when poor sweet Mary travels home it'll be too late and the child'll have to look for a room on her own or in a wretched hostel."

"Come Liz you could put the girl up at a pinch what?"

"I might have my own plans Richard."

"General post eh?"

"I don't know what you mean" she said in a stern voice.

"I say" he exclaimed. "Dreadfully sorry and all. It was nothing."

"That's better" she agreed, smiled sweetly at the man.

Now that the meal was done Miss Jennings got up from table to switch on lights and draw curtains to hide heavy rain pouring down outside. He rose to help. As she straightened the heavy folds he came behind, turned her with a hand on her shoulder and kissed the woman hard on the lips.

"Here" she cried drawing back. "What's this?"

"Oh nothing Liz."

"I like that after all we've discussed." She gaily laughed. "Anyone would think you'd taken our little gossip seriously."

"Must have been this excellent meal you've just given us" he grumbled in a goodhumoured voice.

"That's better" she approved, patted his cheek and led the way next door to the sitting room.

AT THE WEEKEND John Pomfret asked Mrs Weatherby round for drinks at his place. When he had settled her in, she immediately began.

"My dear isn't it absurd and wrong the way those two flaunt themselves nowadays all over London?"

"Now Jane their engagement hasn't been announced yet, at least in the papers, and for all we know it may never happen but there can be no earthly reason why they shouldn't have a little time together to make up their minds, all the more so since I believe Mary is really off to Florence at last."

"You are sweet" Mrs Weatherby pronounced with marked indulgence. "I was speaking of Richard and Liz of course."

"Don't be absurd Jane!"

"D'you actually pretend you hadn't heard my dear?" she cried. "Why I thought everybody knew!"

"Knew what?"

"Just that they've started the most tremendously squalid affair. In one way I'm so glad for Richard, even if I do pity the dear idiot."

"Nonsense" he said. "I don't believe a word. And why are you glad?"

"You ask simply anyone" she replied. "But as to Richard in some respects he's even dearer to me than myself. I'd give almost anything to see the sweet man happy."

"Then is Liz the only future for his happiness?"

"John dear you are so acute. D'you know I'm really rather afraid she is."

"I thought his allegiance was elsewhere" Mr Pomfret suggested and gazed hard at Mrs Weatherby.

"Oh no" she admitted with a cheerful look. "All that became over and done with ages back. Isn't it dreadful?" she giggled.

"Could you be having a game with me Jane?"

She grew serious at once.

"Me?" she asked. "I wish I were." She watched him. "Why" she said after a pause "d'you mind so dreadfully?"

"I?" he demanded and seemed to bluster. "Been expecting it for weeks."

"Well then" she sighed.

"But why can't people come and tell one themselves when they've had enough?" he asked. "Not that you yourself did so with me more years ago than either of us probably cares to remember."

"Now John don't be disagreeable. Besides I was such a giddy young fool in those days."

"A very beautiful creature whatever you may have been" he gallantly said.

"Oh darling" she wailed "just don't remind me of how I look now!"

"You haven't altered at all" he protested. "Why do you speak as though you could ever be a woman my age."

"Because I see you such a lot perhaps" she said.

"Good God if what you say is true well I don't feel as if I shall be able to speak to Liz again. And with due respect to you I can't seem able to think of her with Dick Abbot. Why I should have thought he'd have one of his choking fits."

"Don't be silly John" Mrs Weatherby cried in a delighted voice. "Besides for all we know he may have had several over her already, poor sweet."

Mr Pomfret laughed with some reluctance.

"Really Jane" he protested "what you could ever have seen in that pompous ass I shall never comprehend."

"Speak for yourself darling" she said. "And when I take you in hand, if I find time, you're going to lead a far more regular life let me tell you. Which reminds me. How are you in yourself?"

"Oh I still go for these tests and they give me the injections and I have to wear a little tag round my neck like during the war."

"Is there much in the injection part?"

"Nothing at all. Falling off a log!"

"John you're being so sensible and I do value you so very much. And have you any more news of the children?"

"Not so far as I can tell. I never seem to come across Mary for a chat these days."

"Ever since you put to her your idea she should go to Myra in Florence?"

"My idea Jane? I thought that was your suggestion."

"I still think it such a wise notion of yours John to give the dear girl time to look about. But isn't Mary a little bit rash to throw up her job?"

"Well once they are to marry and will insist they must live on what they earn she might in time have to find a better paid one if Philip can't bring in more."

"Ah we shall have to wait and see" Mrs Weatherby replied. "You are so practical! Still you do think she is going?"

"As far as I know."

"Doesn't she discuss it with you then John? How very wicked and ungrateful of Mary!"

"Oh she hasn't much reason to be grateful has she? No she's talked everything over with Liz."

"Don't be absurd my dear, why that girl has to thank you for all she's got. And I'm really very surprised she should go to dear Liz. What Liz might dig up to say could hardly be disinterested, would it?"

"Well Mary went round to Arthur as you know Jane."

"To Arthur Morris? But . . ." and Mrs Weatherby gaped at him.

"Hadn't you heard? It was she found him dead."

The tears after a moment streamed down Jane's face. She might have been able to cry at will or it could be that she dreadfully minded.

"No John no . . ." she spluttered, struggling with a handkerchief. "It's been such a shock . . . you mustn't . . . poor Arthur . . . oh isn't everything cruel!"

She covered her face and broke into sobs.

"Now darling now" he said coming across to sit on the arm of her chair. He put an arm round Mrs Weatherby, took firm hold on a soft shoulder. "You mustn't let it get you down" he said. "Poor old fellow he didn't suffer, remember that. There dear . . ."

He sat in silence while her upset subsided. After a few minutes she excused herself and went along to the bathroom. He lit a cigarette. He waited. When she returned her fresh face wore a peculiarly vulnerable look.

"Do please excuse me darling" she announced, entering as once before like a ship in full sail. "It was because you see he was alone when it happened!!" She swallowed prodigiously. "But I can never in all my life mention this again! You do understand?"

"Of course."

She settled back in her chair.

"Philip said anything of late?" Mr Pomfret enquired.

"No. What about?"

"This engagement of theirs."

"No" she repeated. She paused. "John my dear" she began "sometimes I rather wonder if we don't discuss the children much too often. After all they have their own lives to lead and that at least we can't do for them! So I've simply given up asking. Do you mind?"

"Whatever you say Jane" he agreed and they settled down to a long nostalgic conversation about old times, excluding any mention of Arthur Morris.

WHEN THE DAY'S WORK was over Philip Weatherby called on Miss Jennings. She answered the door and said,

"Philip! Really you should not drop in on people like this in London!"

"I'm so sorry why not?"

"Because they might be occupied that's why. Never mind, come along."

"Then you are free?"

"I always am to you" she replied, waving him into the flat.

"I wanted to ask what you thought about all this?" he asked, turning round in the door of the living room.

"All what?" she asked from the passage.

"Why Mary and me you know" he answered, and made himself comfortable in the best armchair.

"How d'you mean exactly?" she wanted to be told as she fetched the half finished bottle of sherry.

"Well Liz" he said with assurance, "I look on you as almost one of the family."

"Yes" she replied "I'm nearer your age than your mother ever will be."

"I don't know" he said. "All I wished to ask was, are you on my side or not?"

"Well thanks very much" she retorted drily. "Now would you like a glass of sherry?"

"I wouldn't mind."

"You'll find one day" she put forward "it's odd how like their fathers some sons are."

"But you'd never met Daddy."

"No perhaps I hadn't."

"Then d'you mean . . . ?"

"Now Philip are you going to have a glass of this or no? I'm not here to argue will you understand."

"So sorry" he agreed at once. "I meant I'm in rather a hole with my own personal affairs and as you're a distinct friend of the family's I wanted to get your point."

"In what way?" she asked pouring the wine neatly out.

"About Mary and me" he said.

"Why of course I wish you the very best of everything" she replied.

"Well thanks" he murmured and seemed doubtful. "But does my mother do you think?"

"Jane? She dotes on you Philip. What makes you ask?"

"And Mary's father? I believe you see quite a bit of him. How does he look on us both?"

"Dear John? Now you mustn't assume every sort of silly thing Philip. You don't imagine he discusses the two of you with me do you? Oh he may have done simply ages back but he's stopped. He's not that sort of man that's all."

"I wish I could see my way through" Mr Weatherby complained almost fretfully.

"How d'you mean?"

"No one tells me anything" he said.

"What d'you want them to do Philip quite?"

"Explain to me the way they feel" he elaborated. "When I went to Uncle Ned he wouldn't say a word."

"But what d'you expect them to feel?"

"After all" the young man said "when you go and get engaged you don't just look for silence. It makes one wonder. Does Mary's father approve or doesn't he?"

"Has it ever occurred to you Philip that more than half the time John may just be wondering about himself?"

"Well naturally. But he can spare half a thought to his own daughter can't he?"

"In what way?"

"How do you mean? It's her marriage isn't it?"

"He might be thinking of his own affairs mightn't he?"

"Mr Pomfret? At his age? Why he's a million."

"Good heavens" she said "how old d'you imagine I am?"

"Then you don't mean . . . ?"

"I certainly don't" she replied with finality. "All I say is everyone has a right to their own lives haven't they?"

"In what way?" he enquired.

"You're one of these talkers Philip" she announced. "You don't go out and do things."

"I may not but I work surely?"

"Well there's more to life than working for the Government."

"I don't see what you're getting at" he objected. "How

you spend your day is a part of your life, you can't get away from it."

"But Philip one's evenings are a means to get right apart from what you and I have to do for a living in the daytime."

"D'you know" he said "I can't see why."

"Then oughtn't you to go into politics Philip?"

"I might at that."

"Oh no my dear" she protested "you're hopeless."

"I've got no chance?" he cried.

"I didn't say so at all. What you and Mary decide is none of my concern. You've simply got to take the plunge, there you are, and hope for the best."

"Without Mamma's consent?"

"Why yes Philip if needs be. Doesn't Mary see this my way?"

"I'm not sure. I haven't much experience of women. That's the reason I came round if you want to know."

"You're not asking me to give that to you?" she asked and he blushed. "I'm sorry Philip" she went on. "Forget it. But the truth is I fancy there's going to be another wedding in your family soon if I'm not very much mistaken."

"You and Mr Pomfret d'you mean?"

"Since when were you two related? At any rate you haven't married Mary yet have you?"

"I see you're against Mary and me as well" he said.

"I'm not" she protested. "But you've no right to link my name with John's. What on earth d'you know about it? Of course I'm not going to marry him ever, not that he's asked me. Grow up, be your age for mercy's sake. All I was trying to say is he'll wed your mamma or bust."

"My mother! He can't! She's too old!!"

"No older than he is."

"You can't be serious."

"I am Philip. Never more so."

"Will they want a double wedding then?"

"With Mary and you? Listen Philip if you take my advice you'll rush that nice girl off to the Registry Office always supposing she'll still have you, and get the fell deed done without a word more said to a soul."

"But that wouldn't be straight" he objected and after a good deal more of this sort of argument during which however Liz became somewhat nicer to him, Philip Weatherby took himself away no nearer a decision, or so it seemed.

IN A FEW DAYS TIME Mrs Weatherby again had John Pomfret to dinner following which, after a gay discussion of generalities all through the meal, she led the man into the next room to settle him over a whisky and soda, and immediately began,

"Oh my dear isn't it too frightful about one's money."

"I know" he moaned.

"John even little Penelope's overdrawn now!"

He roared with laughter while she smiled.

"No Jane you can't mean that? Not at her age!"

"But yes" the mother insisted. "Only a trifle of course, the tiny sum a great aunt left the little brigand for her beautiful great eyes. Yet she had a letter from the bank manager Tuesday. I read it out to Pen and we both simply shrieked, she has such a sense of humour already. Still it is dreadful isn't it?"

Mrs Weatherby did not seem greatly disturbed.

"Well Jane" Mr Pomfret beamed "she's started young there's no getting away from that."

"I wish everything didn't go on so" she continued. "Oh John I went to see the awful Mr Thicknesse again who makes me quake in my shoes whenever I meet him like one of those huge things at the Zoo."

"Yes I suppose we must have a talk about the children some time" Mr Pomfret said without obvious enthusiasm.

"No no, damn the children if you'll please excuse the expression. Just for tonight let's be ourselves. I mean we still have our own lives to lead haven't we? No but what is one to do with these Banks?"

"Exactly what I ask myself three or four times a week."

"I never learned to cook, isn't it terrible, and if I started now I'd be so extravagant you see. Honestly I believe I save by having darling Isabella. With the price things are, you can't play about with what little food you do get can you?"

"I'll fry an egg with anyone but not much else" he said.

"And then there's Pen. Even if darling Mother never saw I had cooking lessons she did at least leave me an inkling of essentials from her beloved sweet example, so I do realise it's no earthly use to experiment over a growing child's food. Once I started that I wouldn't be playing the game with my little poppet would I?"

"Oh quite" he agreed, relaxed and smiling.

"So what is one to do?" she demanded. "Just go on in the old way until there's nothing left?"

"I decide and decide to make a great change in my life but I always seem to put it off" he said.

"Don't I know darling!" she cried. "Oh I don't say that to blame, I spoke of myself. But those children we've agreed not to mention John, have changed my ideas. I believe my dear I'm almost beginning to have a plan!"

"Never start a hat shop" he advised. "They invariably fail."

"You are truly sweet" she commented with a small frown which he did not appear to notice. "You see it wasn't that at all, something quite different. The simplest little plot imaginable. Only this. Two people live cheaper than one! They always have and will."

"You're not to take in a lodger Jane" he said sharply.

"But mine is a very especial sort of one" she murmured. "He's you!"

Mr Pomfret sat bolt upright. There was a pause.

"Look here you know" he protested at last "you've got to consider how people'll talk."

"I can't think of the sort of person you imagine I'm like now" she said. "We'd have to be married of course."

There was another longish pause while they watched each other. At last a half smile came over his face.

"And Penelope?" he asked.

"Why she dotes on you John" Mrs Weatherby cried.

"You know what you've told me ever since that unfortunate affair when I married her in front of the fire here?"

"Don't be absurd darling. This is real. Besides it's me who's marrying you, remember. The sweet saint would never even dare to deny her own mother anything."

"But didn't she get very worked up over Mary and Philip?"

"This is precisely what will put all that right out of her sainted little mind don't you see? Oh John do agree you believe me!" Mrs Weatherby cried.

"Of course if you say so Jane, about Pen. Yet you did once just hint how jealous she was."

"Then she'll simply have to get over it" the mother replied with evident disappointment in her lovely voice. "In any case I'd, oh, pondered sending her away to boarding school. She's young but I've begun to think it's time."

He came over, sat by her side on the sofa, and took her hand.

"You're wonderful my dear" he said softly.

"Oh John how disagreeable" she murmured. "So you don't feel you can? Is that it?"

"I hadn't said so. Then do you wish a double wedding?"

"Certainly not. Never!"

He kissed her hand.

"And Mr Thicknesse?" he enquired.

"Oh John you're laughing at me!"

"I'm not" he said and squeezed her hand hard. "I've been over this so often in my mind! But couldn't it be rather late in the day?"

She tried to draw away but he held her fast.

"So you think I'm too old now?" she protested in a low voice.

"That's the last thing Jane. If you only knew how often I'd dreamed of this."

"Oh you have!"

"Yes again and again."

"When?" she demanded with more confidence it seemed.

"Here there and everywhere" he replied.

"Only that?" she reproached him.

He gently kissed a round cheek.

"And Dick?" he whispered.

She jerked away.

"Really" she said "it's too much. You are almost becoming like my Philip."

"I'm sorry Jane."

"But there's nothing, there never has been anything between me and poor dear Richard."

"Yes darling" he agreed.

"So what?" she demanded.

He kissed her on the mouth. She kissed him back almost absentmindedly.

"Will you?" she asked.

"Yes darling" he replied.

"You mean to say you've actually asked me to marry you after all these years?" she crowed, taking his face between her hands and beginning to kiss his eyes.

"I have" he answered half smothered, and plainly delighted.

"But this is wonderful!" she cried.

After an interval during which they kissed, held one another at arm's length, looked fondly on each other and kissed again Mr Pomfret exclaimed,

"I can't hardly believe everything."

"Nonsense, don't say that John. Think how much more it means to me."

"You? Anyone would be proud to marry you!"

179

"Ah how little you know my dear. But there is one matter" she warned, drawing a little away for the last time. "We aren't to have the old days over again if you please. You'll have to give up Liz."

"I never knew her then" he protested.

"I know that already" she said. "I mean now."

"Well of course" he promised. "We hardly ever saw one another anyway except at Sunday lunch and that was only because I was sure to see you there."

"It was!" she cried. "No how truly sweet! Not that I believe you!"

He laughed. "We're going on like an old married couple already" he propounded.

"Who is?" she demanded. "Speak for yourself my sweet old darling. Oh you'll have to look out now!"

"Oh Lord Jane have I said the wrong thing?"

"I should say so" she answered and then she giggled. "But there I expect you'll learn in time. Not that you'll get any other alternative will you, except to be taught by me I mean?"

"I suppose not. Back to school is it?"

"Oh yes yes" she murmured beginning to kiss him again.

He spent the night with her, whispering part of the time because of Philip Weatherby, but they had no more serious conversation.

THE NEXT SUNDAY John Pomfret took Mrs Weatherby to lunch at the hotel and was shown to the table he had been given so often when entertaining Liz. As he sat down he looked round and saw Dick Abbot playing host to Miss Jennings, again at the very spot where Jane had so often been a guest of the man's.

"See who's here" Mr Pomfret invited Mrs Weatherby.

"Oh, don't I know it" she sighed and kept her eyes lowered. "I spotted that couple John as soon as we came in and was so afraid you'd go over with that heavenly goodheartedness of yours."

However he waved in their direction upon which Jane had to turn round, put on a look of great surprise and blow two kisses. Richard and Miss Jennings replied with rather awkward smiles.

"Can't cut 'em anyway" Mr Pomfret muttered.

"There," Mrs Weatherby laughed "we've almost got through that and dear me I was so dreading it!"

"Don't smile Jane for heaven's sake" he implored "or they'll imagine we're laughing at them."

"I could cock a snook at her, the horrid creature" she replied "only I'd never do anything to upset sweet Pascal."

"Oh well if they set up house together, that rather lets you and me out surely."

"Speak for yourself" she said grinning at him. "I haven't a bad conscience."

"Which means you don't have one at all" he laughed.

"I expect yours may be just as clever" she answered.

In the meantime Liz was protesting vigorously to her companion.

"But it disgusts one Richard that's all. To flaunt themselves like this! I asked you particularly to bring me today just in case they might be here. Looking down their noses at each other, simpering like mad."

"Careful now" he said.

"I don't know we've anything to be careful about. Not us!"

"Don't want them to crow."

"Oh they'll do that in any case Richard."

"Then we'd better quickly crow over them."

"So what am I to do?" she smiled. "Stick my poor tongue out at John?"

"When did you get your letter?"

"Three days ago."

"Got mine twenty-four hours before yours at that rate Liz."

"Which only goes to prove he's under her thumb completely. Can't you just hear Jane nagging at him to find out if he'd written yet?"

"Military discipline eh? Oh well I don't suppose a bit of that again'll hurt him."

"A taste of the old Scrubs more likely" she replied with a pure and apparently genuine Cockney intonation. He glanced curiously at her.

She beamed on Mr Abbot.

"My darling" she said. "I almost rather feel I may have had the most miraculous escape."

"How's that?"

"But haven't you often noticed the way some people seem doomed to bring terrible great trials on themselves? Dear old John, I can admit now, is just one of those."

"You're arguing against yourself Liz."

"How dear?"

"You meant Jane would be his trouble didn't you?"

"Well who else? Saving your presence of course."

"And was he also doomed when he kept company with you?"

She laughed.

"How about yourself then, now darling?" she demanded.

"Prefer to choose my own disaster" he replied.

"And have you?"

"Looks very much like" he agreed. She laughed delightedly.

"Oh I'm truly beginning to feel as if I'd escaped" she cried.

"Careful Liz, they'll think we're despising 'em."

"Well aren't we?"

"I'm not."

"Oh cheer up Richard. They can't eat us."

"No but we should keep things in decent order" he explained.

"Whatever you say my dear" she agreed. "Mayn't I even smile?"

"You've got a lovely smile Liz."

"Good heavens a compliment at long last and from you Richard! Now I don't wish to pry but how exactly did Jane write, when you know, what we've just been talking about?"

"Four days ago you mean?"

"When else?"

"Why d'you want to be told Liz?"

"Because of course I'd like to find out if she dictated John's letter."

"Couldn't say" he objected.

"To compare yours with the one John wrote me" she explained.

"Compare notes" he said with no apparent enthusiasm. "I'm not sure Liz. I mean we were both given our marching orders in those letters weren't we. If we put our heads together it might be like a dog going back to his own sick almost."

"Don't be disgusting! I'd like to be sure, that's all."

"But of what?"

"Why Richard I explained. To make certain Jane told him every word to say."

"Oh I don't know Liz" he temporised.

"I don't know about you I agree" she rallied him. "Of course long before I'd received this ridiculous screed from John I'd told the man till I was blue in the face that it could be no go between us where I was concerned and what he wrote really only took notice that at last he'd had to admit I was right."

"Never was good enough for Jane" Mr Abbot admitted with a show of reluctance.

"My dear Richard sometimes you actually fish for compliments."

"I'm not, on my honour."

"Oh yes you are and on this occasion you'll be unlucky. All I'll say is, you may never recover from the shock of Jane Weatherby throwing you over and your life may be finished."

He laughed. "Oh well" he said.

"That's better" she laughed. "So now what?"

"They don't look too cheerful at that do they?" he observed, watching the other couple.

"Oh they won't find it all a bed of roses" she assured Mr Abbot. Upon which she saw Pascal hurry towards John Pomfret's table.

"Watch this" Liz begged Dick Abbot.

"Don't stare too hard" Abbot implored.

"Ah Madame and Mr Pomfret" Pascal cried in his voice which did not travel beyond the table he addressed. "So great my pleasure to me Madame. It is so long since Madame and Monsieur lunch together here on this day like this."

"Pascal!" Mrs Weatherby cried in turn and her tones carried so that one or two looked up from their meals near by. She reached a jewelled right hand across to where he stood bent forward and he took it. Her great eyes seemed to melt. "Why are all the happiest hours of my life bound up with you here Pascal?" she almost purred.

He bowed. "You are too kind" he said. "And is everything as you wish Mrs Weatherby?"

"More than you'll ever know" she answered.

"Then can one hope?" the man began and paused to let go of her hand with a pleasing appearance of regret. "My English is still not so good . . ." he went on. "Can we look forward to many of these luncheons with you and Mr Pomfret Madame?"

"I think so, yes Pascal" Jane beamed upon him.

"Because you understand it makes like old days to see Monsieur here again with Madame." At which he bowed once more and withdrew dexterously backwards with his startling gaze fixed on the lady as though he might never see another promise of heaven.

"Oh John I do feel very happy" Mrs Weatherby exclaimed in a low voice. John Pomfret could see tears in her eyes. "Oh darling isn't it nice that everyone cares about us?"

He smiled with evident affection. "Pascal knows" he announced.

"Of course he does!"

"But how Jane, so soon?"

"From my face naturally you great stupid" she laughed and got the mirror out of her bag to study her great eyes. Under the table he pressed Mrs Weatherby's ankles between his own. "Don't you think I look different? My dear my skin is a new woman's."

"Nonsense" he said lovingly "it always was."

"Oh I do sometimes thank God you're blind and I pray you'll keep so."

"My eyes are all right Jane."

"They're beautiful ones" she assured him "and beautifuller still while they don't know what they miss by staring at me with your particularly sweet expression."

"Why?" he asked with a smile and began to look about him. "Am I missing a lovely girl?"

She laughed and then she sighed. "There you go again, hopeless!" she said with great indulgence. "But I do love you so" she added "although you can tease me so dreadfully!"

A FEW DAYS LATER Philip Weatherby came back to the flat after work to find his mother alone over a finished cup of tea.

"I say Mamma" he began "what's this about Mary throwing up her job?"

"I wouldn't know dear. She never talks much to me."

"I thought Mr Pomfret might've mentioned, perhaps?"

"Philip" his mother said equably "when will you realise that John and I could have other topics besides Mary and yourself."

"Sorry" he put in at once. "I just had a thought."

"Would you mind if she did?" Mrs Weatherby enquired in a lazy way.

"Be quite surprised that's all."

"Why?"

"I don't know really except our work does seriously mean something to us. Not like Mr Pomfret with his absolutely endless complaints every time you meet him."

"Perhaps he's been at his task longer dear" the mother said. "Anyway I do wish you wouldn't stay quite so critical of my friends as you've seemed to lately. What's come over you?"

"Am I being tiresome? I apologise. It's just that I don't appear to know what's going on around any more much. Nobody tells me a word nowadays."

"I do."

As he leant against the fireplace he smiled down on her in what might have been a superior manner.

"Oh you're different" he assured Mrs Weatherby.

"But what makes you wonder about Mary throwing the job up when only a few weeks ago you stood there and told me you didn't care to marry the poor girl?"

"Did I go so far? I'd forgotten. I don't think I'd quite say it now Mamma."

"Well Philip for all your generation being so serious while we're just flighty in your eyes, you certainly seem to have more difficulty in making up your minds than we do."

"Oh come" he replied. "Are you fair? Couldn't it be at my age that one has more opportunities, and anyway we don't have responsibility yet."

"Yes" she sighed "I expect you're right. I didn't mean to

be nasty Philip. Yet things do still happen to my generation you understand."

"They certainly would to you if you let them?".

"What are you insinuating now Philip?"

"Just that you look more like a sister than my mother. I bet you could marry again whenever you wanted."

"You're very sweet" she approved. "As a matter of fact, and I spoke of this before, I've a good memory and I remember it very well, I actually am about to marry again, so there you are."

She turned a radiant and delightfully embarrassed blushing smile on her son who said, "And I haven't forgotten the mess I fell into when I asked you who. I suppose I mustn't try to find out now?"

"To tell the utter truth Philip" she admitted "I was not quite straight with you then, just for the once. Darling you must please be glad but it's my angel John Pomfret."

"Well I say! Oh splendid! When's the ceremony to be?" he burst out, then a sort of cloud seemed to cross his face and his voice dropped. "But now look here Mamma will there be a double wedding? Would Mary like that?"

"She can have whatever she says" Mrs Weatherby said, steadfast.

"And Uncle Ned? Is he pleased?"

Jane moved smartly on the sofa to get a cigarette.

"I don't know and I couldn't care less Philip. Oh my dear boy do rid yourself, oh do, of this family complex!"

"I'm really sorry. I'll try and remember" he promised.

"All the more so when there are mercifully so few of them left" Mrs Weatherby added.

"That might be one of the principal reasons you see" her son pointed out. "But never mind. I say though this is marvellous! Have you broken it to Pen yet?"

"Oh my dear promise me you won't so much as breathe a single word. D'you think I ought to get hold of some doctor to tell her, not Dr Bogle of course? And Philip we ought even to speak of this now in whispers." She suited the action to the word. "Isabella listens at keyholes I'm almost certain, then tells Pen in an Italian only those two can understand; but isn't she simply miraculously clever, darling Penelope!"

He laughed. "I promise" he said.

"Don't you think it the most dreadful thing you've ever heard and in one's own house, each word noted down but what can one do, she's such a marvellous cook dear and my little growing love does benefit so from that?"

"You know Mamma Isabella's English is far too bad."

"Don't you be sure while Pen's teaching the woman our sacred language all the time. Oh but we shall never get at the whole truth. I often think we're not here below to find that out ever, till I believe the truth's even stopped having any importance for me in the least. Which is not to say I go about all day telling lies myself, you're my witness! No I meant generally. But Philip darling do promise you are pleased over John?"

"Of course I am. And have you told Mary?"

"My dear that must be for her Father! And don't you dare breathe a word to the sweet creature till he's spoken."

"Oh quite" Philip promised. "I'll be most discreet."

"You swear!"

"Well naturally Mamma, anything connected with you!"

"You're sure? You're quite certain? Because I'd simply die! If she heard before the proper time I mean!"

"Whatever you say darling" he reassured her and smiled so it seemed with all his heart upon his mother. After which they discussed Bethesda Nathan and soon went off to bed.

THAT SAME EVENING Mr Pomfret had tea with his daughter in their flat.

"I don't know what you'll think of me darling" he began "but the fact is I really might marry once more this time."

"I know Daddy" she smiled. "You've said before."

"But not who" he insisted.

"I've learned never to ask again" she replied. "Can I now though?"

"Well I suppose you'll make out I'm a fool at my age Mary, it's Jane."

"Now how wonderful!" she cried with every appearance of genuine enthusiasm. "Oh I'm so glad for you!" She kissed him.

"You truly are?"

"Of course I am Daddy. And when's it to be?"

"Tell you the truth" he said, still with some embarrassment "we haven't quite got down to dates yet. Are you absolutely sure you're pleased?"

"But of course" she assured him and seemed altogether whole hearted. Then she started frowning. "D'you promise you haven't tried to get me out of the way for the wedding?"

"My dear child what on earth do you mean?"

"The Italian business" she said.

"I don't follow, monkey."

"Why you remember you were so keen I should throw up my job and go out to Italy?"

"Oh that! I swear to you I hadn't even considered it."

"You hadn't!"

"Well this thing about my marriage wasn't on the cards then."

"But you do want me at the ceremony Daddy?"

"Naturally! What sort of a father d'you imagine I am? Couldn't you fly back?"

"That's all right then. All the same why did you wish me away?" she asked.

"It's simply . . ." he began when she interrupted.

"Oh all right" she cried smiling once more. "Whatever

will you think? Here's you getting married and I have to talk about myself!"

"Then you don't find the idea disloyal?"

"Daddy!" she brought out with a dazzling grin. "That's something must be entirely between you and your conscience."

"So you do" he reluctantly put forward.

"I said nothing of the sort" she protested.

"You see it's never easy to explain . . ." he tried once more.

"I didn't suppose it was" she agreed. "Lord there was me a few weeks back trying to tell about Philip and now the roles are properly reversed" she cried. "You're the one stuttering and stammering now" she said.

"I've meant to ask about Philip, Mary . . ."

"No" she cut in on him "this is not the moment. Let's talk about you darling."

"You are sweet" he said. "How can I oblige? What d'you wish to know?"

"Well all of it of course! And right from the beginning."

"Oh that's rather a long story" he objected.

"Whatever you say" she agreed. "So we'll keep everything for another time, very well." Then her face clouded over. "And where d'you both propose to live?" she demanded.

"I'm not sure my love. We hadn't really considered that yet. Wherever will be cheapest of course" he added with the whine of a guilty conscience in his voice. "In fact" he went on "Jane has been making pretty much of a point how things come cheaper for two people than they do for one."

"Oh I'd have to find somewhere else naturally" she admitted with what seemed to be amused if guarded acquiescence.

"Why good Lord monkey you surely wouldn't think we'd turn you out! Besides there's your own future to consider. No the little I meant was it's less expensive for three in one flat than to live split up in two of them."

"And there's Philip, and Penelope."

"Well yes so there is! Bless me we may have to take a larger place that's all. And while we're about it we might move to a less disgusting neighbourhood than what Jane and I both live in now. I must speak to Jane. Because the way this particular quarter has gone down lately is too frightful."

"I shouldn't bank on Philip and me setting up shop so very soon Daddy."

"Why what are you trying to tell now dear?"

"Very little. Anyway don't let's talk about me just this minute. Today belongs to you. It was only for when you make your plans, that's why I said what I did. Anyway I'll have to get a room of my own. But still, enough of that darling."

"However you wish Mary."

"Well doesn't everything seem very strange to you?" she demanded. "Your going to be married I mean?"

"Oh my love I'm so worried about dear Penelope!" he brought out at once.

"Yes Daddy?"

"She needs a man in the house."

"Have a heart! She's not seven yet."

"I've such a responsibility towards Jane regarding the poor child" Mr Pomfret insisted. "There's no getting away from it, cardinal errors have been made with that little thing. She's just a mass of nerves. I owe this to Jane to get her right."

His daughter laughed, not unkindly. "Pen will be a match for every one of you I'm afraid."

"No monkey I'm serious" Mr Pomfret declared. "Marriage has certain responsibilities as you'll find in due course when your time comes. I've taken on quite a lot where Penelope's concerned."

"Oh I'd be inclined to agree with you there Daddy."

He laughed a bit shamefacedly in return for the broad smile she gave him.

"Am I being ridiculous again?" he asked.

"Perhaps you are just a little" she replied. "Well now I ought to go out and meet Philip. Goodbye for now darling" she said and kissed him hard. "I wish you every single thing you deserve and you're wonderful" she ended.

"You'll have me crying like Pen in two twos" he laughed.

MARY JOINED Mr Weatherby in the bar of the public house they always used in Knightsbridge.

"Sorry I'm late" she excused herself. "My father was making his announcement."

"So he's told you" the young man said and pushed one of two glasses of light ale towards her. "Seems rather extraordinary that they could marry!"

"Well why shouldn't they?"

"After knowing each other all those years!" he objected. "When we're engaged?"

"I'd not be too certain if I were you" she said looking away from him.

"Why how do you mean?" he demanded.

"Just what I say Philip."

"No one tells one anything" he complained. "Are you trying to make out we're not to be married any more?"

"You know Daddy wants me to go to Italy?"

"How does that really alter our plans?" he asked.

"I simply can't apply for leave from the Department for any length of time" she answered as she twiddled her glass of beer round and round on the table and watched it closely. "It's rather sweet in one regard if you wish to know" she added. "He'd prefer me away to let him get adjusted, I'm sure that's why."

"Mary I don't follow you at all."

"Well put yourself in their position, or in my father's if you like! He's embarrassed of course he must be, marrying an old flame at his age. He doesn't care to have a grown daughter around while he adjusts himself to your mother, and marriage is tremendously a matter of adjustment you must admit Philip."

"I never said it wasn't did I?"

"Quite. I'm glad you agree. Which will make everything so much easier. For you know we've got to have a bit of a talk you and I one of these days."

"What about for heaven's sake?"

"Everything Philip."

"Oh dear" he cried, but with a smile "this does sound ominous of you!"

"I don't know" she answered. "All I am almost sure of is you won't mind."

"You're giving me marching orders?" he enquired as he watched the toe of his shoe.

"I might be, yes" she replied.

"You mean to say you aren't absolutely certain?" he asked with a sort of detachment. She turned to face Mr Weatherby.

"Philip you mustn't laugh!" she warned.

"I'm not" he assured her with a straight face.

"For a minute I thought you were" she admitted and from the tone of her voice she could have been near to tears. "I'm not sure you mayn't even have worked for this" she added.

"In what way?" he demanded.

"Oh why are you so difficult to know Philip?" she asked transferring her attention back to the glass she held and did not drink from. "I think that's the whole trouble. I can't make you out a bit."

"Don't get worked up Mary."

"But part of all I'm trying to tell you is, I'll have to leave the Department; I've just explained I can't ask for extended leave. If they gave it me they'd be bound to take as much off my holiday periods and so in the end I'd never get away again for ages which would be impossible even you will agree Philip."

"Really your Father is the most selfish man" he burst out and raised his voice in indignation. "Entirely because he's bent on marrying my mother all of a sudden, a thing he's not thought of for years, he insists that you throw up a job which is a whole part of your life . . ."

Miss Pomfret interrupted and had to shake his elbow to do so.

"Quiet Philip you'll have everyone listening in a moment. And anyway less of all this about Daddy please!"

"I can't help but . . ."

"No Philip I mean what I say. I never bring up anything against your mother so why should you start about my parent?"

"I wasn't blaming him so much as I was the way he treated you."

"Where's the difference?" she asked.

"Very well then you win" he replied in a calmer voice. "So you're to chuck the whole career up in order to give your father time to get to know Mamma when they've lived in each other's pockets ever since we were born!"

"Go on I'm listening Philip" she commented acidly.

"But dear my only thought is of you!" he protested with what seemed to be some unease.

"Why?" she demanded.

"How why?" he enquired.

"Did you think of me suddenly then?"

"Well Mary isn't that natural?"

"Except this. When you could have done something for me, for us both if you like, you'd insist time and again, Philip, you mustn't upset your family! It's they who've come first always, isn't that so?"

"I don't know what you're referring to" he said.

"You made one great mistake Philip" she explained in hushed tones. "I told you once but you wouldn't listen.

And that was we should have married, then told them all at your mother's beastly party, and only then."

"Now who's being offensive about parents?"

"Oh Philip I only said about the party, I didn't breathe a word against your mother though probably I might have if I tried. No, and now it may be too late!"

"What may be?"

"Our engagement Philip!"

"You don't mean to say you agreed to go through the ceremony with me just to stop our parents' marriage!"

"Don't be disgusting! Of course not."

"See here Mary" he said with what might have been firmness "there's no good in your getting cross. The fact is you're not a bit clear at the moment and I can't make sense out of all you say."

"I meant things might be too late now for us to marry Philip."

"No, look, of course it's for you to decide, but don't rush this! You're all on edge which is only natural. Go to Italy by all means, give yourself a chance to think everything over. But I'm bound to tell you throwing up your job on a whim as you are must affect me. I mean to say, what serious man wouldn't consider, well you know . . . Honestly that does seem childish!"

"There you are!"

"Where am I?" he demanded.

"But you don't think of me in the least, ever" she angrily protested. "If I talk of giving up my job you merely make threats about the effect it will have on you! Not that I care my dear in the least, so there!"

"I was trying to suggest what was best."

"So you believe my interests lie in marrying you Philip?"

"Not at all" he answered warmly. "I've nowt to offer. I've never been able to believe you ever would. From your point of view it must be madness."

"Well well!" she said and smiled on him. "Oh I know you'll think me awful but I must have more time. Still I wish you could have been decided like this all through. Oh Philip I have been miserable, truly I have! At moments."

"I don't suppose anything's been very gay for anyone except our sainted parents" he replied.

"There you go again!" she wearily complained.

"Sorry. Forget it. Now how shall we leave all this? I know you will be annoyed but one thing I do bless my lucky star for, that we didn't put our engagement in the papers. No" and he raised a warning hand at the expression on her face "don't say it! If marriage is a long grind, as they make out, of give and take then my feelings for my family are just one of those bad patches you'll have to get used to. And I warn you there's no one will ever get me out of them. Anyway go to Italy dear and see how you feel when you do come back."

"Oh no Philip" she burst out, turning scarlet, "you're not to be so bloody to me!! Here take your beastly ring, I'm off!"

She almost ran out. He went rather white and cautiously looked round the saloon bar, presumably to see if anyone had noticed. No one appeared to be watching however. After which he finished both light ales and then left with much composure.

"WELL SHE'S GIVEN HIM back the ring Richard" Miss Jennings announced as she opened the door to Mr Abbot.

"Good God, can't have been worth much then!"

"No, no Mary has to Philip, not Jane to John."

"I thought all was settled between those two" he said carefully as he folded his overcoat on a chair. "The children that is at least" he added.

"Why my dear you haven't heard anything about John have you?"

"No Liz but after what's happened to the couple of us nothing in human nature can ever surprise me again."

"You are sweet. I like you so much better when you begin to be cross with Jane and John. And once upon a time I really thought you never would be!"

He coughed and rubbed his hands together before her fire.

"Rotten summer we've had" he said.

"Yes Mary's given him back the ring" Miss Jennings insisted.

"And has Jane had hers yet?" he wanted to be told.

"I don't know. Oh d'you think so? I would really terribly like to see it. Because if he can't do better for Jane than Philip was able to manage for John's daughter the fur will simply fly my dear, you'll see."

"Would she go as far as to chuck the thing back in his face?" Mr Abbot enquired smiling.

"Jane? Why you don't want that surely Richard? Not now any more you can't?"

"Not sure my old wishes will have a great deal to do with anything you know, not where they're concerned anyway."

"Why did you ask in that case?"

"Curiosity never killed a cat in spite of all they say Liz."

"But if you're so curious, then you do still care what happens to Jane! Oh Richard you can give yourself away at times so terribly!"

"Well don't you mind about John?"

"I just won't let myself."

"Nonsense my dear of course you'd like to know if he'd made up his mind not to marry Jane."

"I could still do with a small little satisfaction of my own if that's what you mean" she answered. "But I won't allow myself to care about how the man behaves afterwards."

"Not much between us then probably" he admitted.

197

"Now what are you getting at?" she demanded, smiling with obvious pathos.

"We're in the same boat right enough it seems."

"Then don't you start to rock the thing by yearning after Jane!"

"Oh Liz as I told you once before I'm 'just a thanks a million' old soldier now."

"Well I say it's John should be thankful all his life to me and so should Jane be for you."

"Why?" he asked. "What've we done towards 'em in the long run?"

"But my dear" she cried "I'm ever so clear about it all!" Her voice was genuinely light and gay. "It was we who rendered everything possible for those two, which made me so restless and cross at one time. They'd simply got into the habit of getting old, Jane even gloried in letting herself go, now don't protest, and when she saw I was beginning to make something of John she grew so jealous she just couldn't stand anything."

"Where do I come into it then?"

"Why by being the sweetest man in the whole wide world and so enormously modest you can't even lift a thumb! Don't tell me she'd have been able to carry on once again with John if you'd as much as raised your little finger!"

"Did you let John off without a fight Liz?"

"Oh I'm different" she admitted in honeyed accents. "There's a fate on me Richard darling! Whenever I get involved with a man he always goes back to some first love old enough to be my mother."

"Never heard such poppycock in all my life" he gallantly protested.

"Ah but you don't know, you can't."

"A lovely creature like you" he insisted.

"Then why aren't I married now?"

"Often wondered and then by Jove one day I saw the whole thing in a flash! Fact is Liz you're so damned honest and that's a wonderful quality, rarest thing on earth nowadays! You just frighten 'em off when they can't measure themselves up."

"Richard is this a compliment?"

"Certainly is!"

"If you go on like it you'll make me cry" she beamed upon him. "Because you're the kindest sweetest man I think I've ever met. Oh you'll make a woman so happy one of these days!"

"D'you believe that?" he demanded almost fiercely.

"As much as anything I've ever uttered in my whole life!"

"Because when Jane won't have me I doubt anyone else will now?" he muttered.

"Don't be so absurd! I tell you any woman would be proud and honoured Richard! And what d'you dare to mean by 'now'?"

"I'm no' getting any younger Liz."

"I can't make you out at all" she protested. "D'you feel old?"

"Can't say I do" he replied.

"Well where's the trouble then Richard? As I've told you before but you simply won't listen!"

"I don't remember exactly Liz?"

"Why so far as I'm concerned I prefer older people, older than myself I mean. And you once said such a sweet thing to me when you were on the subject."

"I did? You do?"

"There you go again" she said cheerfully. "Oh I might have known this! Then was it just one of those things you throw off at a party?"

"Dreadfully sorry . . ." he began but she interrupted.

"You should be more careful what you say to women" she complained with a laugh. "You're almost impossible Richard. And I did set such store! You told me at the engagement party what you liked where I was concerned was my special blend of still being young and yet that I'd all the allure of experience."

"Good God I've always felt it Liz."

199

"Then why couldn't you recollect?"

"I did" he insisted. "I do."

"After all that's happened how can I believe you now?" she asked, her back to the fire.

"Never could manage to be much use at explaining" he said, moved over, put his arms about her waist and gave her a hug and a long kiss. She drew back but not away from his arms.

"Oh no you don't!" she laughed upon which he embraced her again.

"Look here . . ." she said seriously when next he allowed her to come up for air but at once his mouth came back on hers. After a moment she went noticeably limp and then, while he still pressed his lips on her tongue she raised her arms and tightened these around his neck.

"Oh Dick!" she said at last. "Oh Dick!!"

Upon which for no discoverable reason he began to choke. He soon had to let go of her and if at first she seemed to smile goodnaturedly, then as his face grew more purple and at last black, as his staring eyes appeared to fight an enemy within so frightful was the look of preoccupation on them, so in no time at all she was thumping his back, breaking off to fetch a glass of water, letting off small "oh's" of alarm until, when his red eyes were almost out of their sockets he began to be able to draw breath once more and what was plainly a glow of ease started to pale him, to suffuse his patient, gentle orbs. Upon which, before this expression had time to grow positively hang dog, she got him in the bedroom on the bed. As he lay watching her and she unbuttoned his collar he found his voice again.

"Dreadfully sorry but quite all right now" he gasped.

"What was it then?" she cried.

"Always have often swallowed the wrong way all my life."

"I was so frightened. Oh Dick!" she said laying her soft cheek along his face.

He stayed the night and next morning she seemed entirely jubilant.

A WEEK OR SO LATER Mrs Weatherby entertained John Pomfret once more at her flat. It was dusk and as they were seated next each other on the sofa, his arm around her shoulders while she held his free hand moist in both of hers; as the fire glowed a powerful rose and it rained outside so that drops on the dark panes, which were a deep blue of ink, by reflection left small snails' tracks across and down the glass in rose, for Mrs Weatherby had not drawn the curtains; as he could outline her heavy head laid next his only in a soft blur with darker hair over her great eye above the gentle fire-wavering profile of her nose, and, because he was nearest to this living pile of coals in the grate, he could see into this eye, into the two transparencies which veiled it, down to that last surface which at three separate points glowed with the fire's same rose; as he sat at her lazy side it must have seemed to him he was looking right into Jane, relaxed inert and warm, a being open to himself the fire and the comfort of indoors but with three great furnaces quiescent in her lovely head just showing through eyeholes to warn a man, if warning were needed, that she could be very much awake, did entirely love him with molten metal within her bones, within the cool back of her skull which under its living weight of hair was deeply, deeply known by his fingers.

"Oh dear" she murmured for the third time "darling d'you think we should close the shutters?"

He did not answer but tightened hold, to keep her. At that she leant a little more against his shoulder.

They had been talking by fits and starts, not so much in

reply one to the other as to make peaceful barely related statements which had advanced very little what they presumably meant by everything they said because they now seemed in all things to agree, in comfort in quiet and rest.

"So you don't feel dearest you should be married in church?" she sighed as though to sum up a long discussion.

"Registry office, or might look ridiculous! At our age" he almost whispered to an ear he could not see.

"However you say" she agreed. There was another pause. "I'll think about it" she added.

"What was that darling?"

"The Registry Office" she explained.

"I know. Go on" he mumbled, yawning.

"I said I'd think it over, aren't you sweet" she sighed again and silence fell once more. After a long pause she murmured,

"D'you realise I can hardly believe Mary's given him back the ring, dearest?"

"Which ring?"

"Why the engagement! You're not to fall asleep on me yet" she commanded in her softest voice.

"Yes she did" he murmured "or so she said." He yawned again.

"But Philip's never mentioned a syllable John."

"Can't hardly think Mary'd actually go as far as pawn the object" he muttered.

"Oh darling the poor child could not get much for what it was, would she" and indolently saying this Mrs Weatherby chuckled. "Oh no she simply's not made that way, Mary'd never do such a thing. Now she's gone to dear Myra in Florence, Philip's taken Bethesda out twice, yes twice, two whole times did you know?"

"Never heard of her. Who's she?"

"So unsuitable dearest, a girl at his work."

"Well Jane" he said with a sort of low-pitched assurance, then yawned a fifth time, "our children will just have to work their own lives out, we can't do everything for them."

She gave no answer. They relapsed into easy silence. After quite an interval he began again,

"But Jane my dear as I've explained before this very evening, I'm worried about your Penelope. I feel I've a real responsibility towards you there darling."

He spoke so softly she could not have heard for she asked, "A real what my heart?"

"Responsibility, love. Always told you a man about the house is what the child needs. Now just when she's going to have a stepfather you speak of sending her off to ah . . ." and he yawned yet once more "to one of those sleeping places, how d'you call 'em . . ." and he came to an end.

"Boarding schools" she gently prompted.

"Yes . . . thick ankles . . . hockey, Jane."

"Oh no the poor angel, then I'd never allow it" the mother protested comfortably but with a trifle more animation.

"There you are . . ." he mumbled. "Always knew you couldn't send her away . . . when things came to the point."

"Oh no" she quietly said "I'd stop her playing those games at school then."

"Expect you know best" he commented, yawning a last time.

There was a longer pause while his eyelids drooped.

"And how's your wicked diabetes my own darling?" she whispered.

"All right" he barely answered.

"And is there anything at all you want my own?"

"Nothing . . . nothing" he replied in so low a voice she could barely have heard and then seemed to fall deep asleep at last.

DALKEY ARCHIVE PAPERBACKS

PIERRE ALBERT-BIROT, *Grabinoulor.*

YUZ ALESHKOVSKY, *Kangaroo.*

FELIPE ALFAU, *Chromos.*

  Locos.

  Sentimental Songs.

ALAN ANSEN,

  Contact Highs: Selected Poems 1957-1987.

DJUNA BARNES, *Ladies Almanack.*

  Ryder.

JOHN BARTH, *LETTERS.*

  Sabbatical.

AUGUSTO ROA BASTOS, *I the Supreme.*

ANDREI BITOV, *Pushkin House.*

ROGER BOYLAN, *Killoyle.*

CHRISTINE BROOKE-ROSE, *Amalgamemnon.*

GERALD BURNS, *Shorter Poems.*

GABRIELLE BURTON, *Heartbreak Hotel.*

MICHEL BUTOR,

  Portrait of the Artist as a Young Ape.

JULIETA CAMPOS,

  The Fear of Losing Eurydice.

ANNE CARSON, *Eros the Bittersweet.*

LOUIS-FERDINAND CÉLINE, *Castle to Castle.*

  London Bridge.

  North.

  Rigadoon.

HUGO CHARTERIS, *The Tide Is Right.*

JEROME CHARYN, *The Tar Baby.*

MARC CHOLODENKO, *Mordechai Schamz.*

EMILY HOLMES COLEMAN,

  The Shutter of Snow.

ROBERT COOVER, *A Night at the Movies.*

STANLEY CRAWFORD,

  Some Instructions to My Wife.

RENÉ CREVEL, *Putting My Foot in It.*

RALPH CUSACK, *Cadenza.*

SUSAN DAITCH, *Storytown.*

PETER DIMOCK,

  A Short Rhetoric for Leaving the Family.

COLEMAN DOWELL, *The Houses of Children.*

  Island People.

  Too Much Flesh and Jabez.

RIKKI DUCORNET, *The Complete Butcher's Tales.*

  The Fountains of Neptune.

  The Jade Cabinet.

  Phosphor in Dreamland.

  The Stain.

WILLIAM EASTLAKE, *Castle Keep.*

  Lyric of the Circle Heart.

STANLEY ELKIN, *Boswell: A Modern Comedy.*

  Criers and Kibitzers, Kibitzers and Criers.

  The Dick Gibson Show.

  The MacGuffin.

  The Magic Kingdom.

ANNIE ERNAUX, *Cleaned Out.*

LAUREN FAIRBANKS, *Muzzle Thyself.*

  Sister Carrie.

LESLIE A. FIEDLER,

  Love and Death in the American Novel.

RONALD FIRBANK, *Complete Short Stories.*

FORD MADOX FORD, *The March of Literature.*

JANICE GALLOWAY, *Foreign Parts.*

  The Trick Is to Keep Breathing.

WILLIAM H. GASS, *The Tunnel.*

  Willie Masters' Lonesome Wife.

ETIENNE GILSON, *The Arts of the Beautiful.*

C. S. GISCOMBE, *Giscome Road.*

  Here.

KAREN ELIZABETH GORDON, *The Red Shoes.*

PATRICK GRAINVILLE, *The Cave of Heaven.*

GEOFFREY GREEN, ET AL., *The Vineland Papers.*

HENRY GREEN, *Concluding.*

  Nothing.

JIŘÍ GRUŠA, *The Questionnaire.*

JOHN HAWKES, *Whistlejacket.*

ALDOUS HUXLEY, *Antic Hay.*

  Point Counter Point.

  Those Barren Leaves.

  Time Must Have a Stop.

GERT JONKE, *Geometric Regional Novel.*

TADEUSZ KONWICKI, *A Minor Apocalypse.*

  The Polish Complex.

ELAINE KRAF, *The Princess of 72nd Street.*

EWA KURYLUK, *Century 21.*

DEBORAH LEVY, *Billy and Girl.*

JOSÉ LEZAMA LIMA, *Paradiso.*

OSMAN LINS, *The Queen of the Prisons of Greece.*

ALF MAC LOCHLAINN,

  The Corpus in the Library.

  Out of Focus.

D. KEITH MANO, *Take Five.*

BEN MARCUS, *The Age of Wire and String.*

WALLACE MARKFIELD, *Teitlebaum's Window.*

  To an Early Grave.

DAVID MARKSON, *Collected Poems.*

  Reader's Block.

  Springer's Progress.

  Wittgenstein's Mistress.

CARL R. MARTIN, *Genii Over Salzburg.*

CAROLE MASO, *AVA.*

HARRY MATHEWS, *Cigarettes.*

  The Conversions.

Visit our website: www.dalkeyarchive.com

DALKEY ARCHIVE PAPERBACKS

Visit our website: www.dalkeyarchive.com